PRAISE FC

"The Gears are the preeminent historical novelists of our times, offering fascinating and brilliantly researched insights into war, suffering, tribal life, and the beliefs that inspire people to act above and beyond what they thought possible. No one reads a Gear novel without being transformed in beautiful ways. The Gears, separately and together, rank among the most significant novelists of modern times, and their work will endure for generations."

— RICHARD S. WHEELER

"The multitalented Gears, husband-and-wife archaeologists and bestselling authors, score a literary bull's-eye as they weave another vivid narrative thread into their stunning tapestry of Native Americans... The Gears continue to do a magnificent job of advancing a fascinating historical chronicle via action, adventure, and archeology."

— *BOOKLIST*

"Rich in cultural detail. Both longtime fans and newcomers will be satisfied. Another fine entry in an ambitious, long-running series."

— *KIRKUS REVIEWS*

SHADOWED FOREST

ALSO BY W. MICHAEL GEAR AND KATHLEEN O'NEAL GEAR

Big Horn Legacy

Dark Inheritance

The Foundation

Fracture Event

Long Ride Home

The Mourning War

Raising Abel

Rebel Hearts Anthology

Sand in the Wind

Thin Moon and Cold Mist

Black Falcon Nation Series

Flight of the Hawk Series

The Moundville Duology

Saga of a Mountain Sage Series

The Wyoming Chronicles

The Anasazi Mysteries

SHADOWED FOREST

THE PEACEMAKER'S TALE
BOOK TWO

W. MICHAEL GEAR

KATHLEEN O'NEAL GEAR

WOLFPACK
PUBLISHING
— EST 2013 —

Shadowed Forest
Paperback Edition
Copyright © 2024 (As Revised) W. Michael Gear and
Kathleen O'Neal Gear

Wolfpack Publishing
701 S. Howard Ave. 106-324
Tampa, Florida 33609

wolfpackpublishing.com

Illustrations by Ellisa Mitchel.

Paperback ISBN 978-1-63977-171-4
eBook ISBN 978-1-63977-170-7

To Tim, Maria, Brandon, and Connor O'Neal, for the sacrifices you made while caring for our mother in her last difficult years. No one could have been kinder, or taken better care of her. We know it wasn't easy. You'll always have a special place in our hearts.

ACKNOWLEDGMENTS

We could not have written the *Peacemaker Saga* series without the dedication and hard work of our archaeological colleagues, many of whom have spent their lives trying to understand the prehistory of this continent. In writing this book, we relied heavily upon the work of Bruce Trigger, Dean Snow, James Tuck, Elisabeth Tooker, William Ritchie, Christina Rieth, John Hart, Mary Ann Levine, Kenneth Sassaman, Michael Nassaney, and Paul Wallace. We are especially grateful to Dr. David Dye, University of Memphis, for his work on prehistoric war and peace movements in the eastern United States.

In addition, the detailed analysis by Barbara Mann and Jerry Fields with regard to dating the founding of the League was very informative. Their article can be found at www.wampumchroni-cles.com/signinthesky.html; it contains a thorough discussion of the historical record and Iroquoian oral history, and provides an excellent cultural context for dating the famed eclipse.

Lastly, we would like to offer our sincere

thanks to Catherine Crumpler, and the Hot Springs County Counseling Center in Thermopolis, Wyoming, for their help in understanding the psychological responses of children undergoing extreme stress. Those lengthy discussions were not wasted, Catherine. Thanks for sharing your expertise.

NON-FICTION
INTRODUCTION

There are eight parts in the Peacemaker Saga. The first four parts, *People of the Longhouse, Shadowed Forest, The Dawn Country,* and *The Dusk Country* will focus on the early lives of two of the most important, and least known, heroes in world history: Dekanawida and Hiyawento.

The last four parts of the Peacemaker Saga will chronicle their later lives, along with telling the story of Jigonsaseh, who can justifiably be called "The Mother of American Democracy."

Without these three people and their struggle for peace in fifteenth-century North America, it's doubtful that any of the ideals we cherish as free people would exist today.

In fact, it's doubtful that The Free World would exist today.

Let's talk about the origins of Northern

Iroquoians; it's is a hotly debated and very complex topic among archaeologists, but generally we agree that the period from roughly AD 1000-1300 demonstrates fluid and shifting alliances, expanding trade networks, and changing settlement patterns. One thing is for certain: Early Iroquoian cultures were remarkably adaptable and diverse.

Most archaeologists divide Iroquoian culture into three periods: The Early Iroquoian period from AD 1000-1300, the Middle Iroquoian period from AD 1300-1350, and Late Iroquoian from AD 1350 to European contact. For the purposes of this introduction, the Early Iroquoian period is particularly important. Not because it was the apogee of the culture—it wasn't—but because something dramatic happened. At around AD 1000, most Iroquoian peoples lived in small fishing villages or farming hamlets, primarily along rivers where they had good fertile soils and easy access to water. Toward the end of this period, they began moving away from watercourses and started building their villages atop easily defensible hilltops. Some were palisaded—for example, the Bates site in Chenango County and the Sackett site near Canandaigua, New York, both of which date to the thirteenth century.

It is also likely that during the Early period, Iroquoian societies changed from being patrilineal and patrilocal—meaning they traced descent through the male, and women came to live with their husband's family—to being matrilineal and matrilocal, in which they traced descent through the female and after marriage a man moved in with his wife's family.

During the thirteenth and fourteenth centuries, the size of Iroquois villages began to grow. Archaeologists call this "population aggregation," meaning that more and more people were crowding together within the palisaded walls of villages. We see these expanded longhouses at places like the Furnace Brook and Howlett Hill sites in New York, where archaeologists excavated houses that were 210 and 334 feet long. This Middle Iroquoian period also saw the people becoming increasingly dependent upon maize-bean-squash agriculture. As in historic times, men probably cleared the fields, built the houses, and hunted, while women were the farmers. They cultivated the soil, planted, tended the fields, harvested and stored the crops. When women began to account for more and more of the food, their lineages also probably became the dominant social avenue for prestige.

At around AD 1400, the first evidence for individual tribes appears. Differences in pottery styles, burial customs, and types of houses demonstrate divisions between Iroquoian groups. As well, small villages begin to amalgamate with larger ones, forming cohesive social groups, or, we suspect, nations.

AD 1400 is also the time when the Iroquois were building the most impressive longhouses, and many were elaborately fortified. At the Schoff site outside Onondaga, New York, the people constructed a longhouse 400 feet long, 22 feet wide, and nearly as tall. The palisaded settlement may have housed 1,500 to 2,000 people, consisting of many different clans.

As those of you who've read our previous books know, often this type of aggregation is a telltale sign for archaeologists of interpersonal violence. Simply put, people crowd together for defensive purposes. This is also when cannibalism first appears in the Iroquoian archaeological record in the form of cut and cooked human bones.

People of the Longhouse takes place at this critical moment in time.

Why did warfare break out? The fact that the climate had grown cooler and drier certainly contributed to the violence. We know that droughts were more frequent, growing seasons shorter, and food shortages probably more common. As well, larger villages deplete resources at a faster rate. Game populations, nut forests, firewood, and fertile soils would all have played out more quickly, which means they must have had to move their villages more often. Moving may have brought them into conflict with neighbors who needed the resources just as desperately.

The warfare, we know, was violent.

At the Alhart site in the Oak Orchard Creek drainage in western New York, archaeologists found evidence of burned longhouses and food, and the dismembered remains of seventeen people —most of them male. Historically, it was common practice for women and children to either be killed on site, or taken captive and marched away while the male warriors were tortured and killed. At this site, the fragments of a child's skull were found in one storage pit, and the skull of a woman in another storage pit. As well, fifteen male skulls were found in a storage pit on top of charred corn, and were probably placed there as severed heads, in the flesh. Some of them were burned. Two had suffered blows to the front of the head.

At the Draper site northeast of Toronto, fourteen burials date to this period. One burial, an old man, was missing both arms and his shoulder blades. A chert arrow point was embedded in his right hip bone—the femoral neck. There was also evidence that he had been speared in the chest, and scalped. As well, he had sustained a severe blow to the left side of his head, and showed cut marks from having been dismembered. Dismembering the enemy was historically a method of stopping the soul from taking revenge upon its killers; dismemberment apparently immobilized the angry spirit of the dead.

The Van Oordt site, a late fourteenth to early fifteenth-century site near Kitchener, Ontario, revealed thirteen burials. One had fragments of three arrow points embedded in his bones. He also showed signs of numerous puncture wounds; which means he was stabbed several times. Then, both of his arms were severed, and he was beheaded.

At the Cameron site near Lima, New York, a young male burial was discovered. He'd been burned, and showed signs of having been stabbed and scalped. Afterward, his skull was broken open, probably to extract the brain. The interesting thing here is that this young man was buried in the village cemetery, not in a refuse midden. This may mean that his body was found by his relatives and brought home for proper burial.

As well, artifacts made from human bone are plentiful on Northern Iroquoian sites that date from the late fourteenth through the early sixteenth centuries. For example, two skulls were found at the Parsons site in Toronto. The Parsons site was an elaborately palisaded fifteenth-century village. The two skulls, one male and one female, were found in a trash pit inside the inner palisade. Many other human bone artifacts are found in similar "refuse" situations. Human skull pendants or rattles are found across Ontario and New York at the Moatfield, Winking Bull, Uren, Pound, Crawford Lake, Jarrett-Lahmer, Draper, Keffer, Lawson, Campbell, Clearview, Parsons, Bee-ton, Roebuck, Lite, Salem, and Glenbrook sites. Often, the skulls, or skull fragments, have cut marks made by stone tools that are suggestive of scalping. As you already know from earlier paragraphs, scalping was not a French custom brought to the New World and adopted by the tribes; it existed long before Europeans arrived. Such skulls were found at the Draper, Keffer, and Lawson sites. Ground and polished fibulas and femurs—leg bones—as well as arm bones—radii—were used for beads and scraping tools. Pierced mandibles—jaws)—and finger and toe bones were used as pendants. Ulnae —arm bones—became awls or daggers, and were also strung as beads. Why is it important to archae-ologists that all these artifacts were found in trash middens? Because Iroquoian peoples took very good care of their dead relatives. They had lengthy and beautiful burial rituals to make certain their loved ones reached the Land of the Dead. Since these human remains were not properly cared for, it suggests the bones may have come from less valu-able members of society, like enemy captives.

Let's take a few moments to discuss the Iroquoian perspective on captives. By the 1400s, as it was in historic times, warfare and raiding for captives was probably the most important method of gaining prestige in Northern Iroquoian societies. When a person died, the spiritual power of the clan was diminished, especially if that person had been a community leader. The places of missing family members literally remained vacant until they could be "replaced," and their spiritual power—which was embodied in their name—transferred to another person.

Historical records tell us that during the 1600s, the Iroquois dispatched war parties whose sole intent was to bring home captives to replace family members and restore the spiritual strength of the clans. These were called "mourning wars." Clan matrons usually organized the war parties and ordered their warriors to bring them captives suitable for adoption to assuage their grief and restock the village. Once the clan had a suitable replacement, the captive underwent the Requickening Ceremony. In this ritual, the dead person's soul was "raised up" and transferred to the captive, along with his or her name.

This may seem odd to modern readers, but keep the religious context in mind. The Iroquois believed that the souls of those who died violently could not find the Path of Souls in the sky that led to the Land of the Dead. They were excluded from the afterlife and doomed to spend eternity wandering the earth, seeking revenge. However, such souls could find rest if they were transferred—along with their name—to the body of another person. In a very concrete way, the relatives of the dead person were trying to save him.

The souls of men and women killed in battles that were not "raised up" were believed, according to some Seneca traditions, to move into trees. It was these trees with indwelling warrior spirits that the People cut to serve as palisade logs, thereby surrounding the village with Standing Warriors.

Who was fighting? We're fairly sure the warfare was between neighbors, not marauding armies seeking out distant enemies. Why? Archaeologists do craniometric analyses—measurements of skulls—and compare them with other populations to determine their differences or similarities, which indicate probable genetic relationships. In 1998, Dupras and Pratte conducted a detailed study of skulls from the Parsons site and compared them with four other groups, two local—from the nearby Kleinberg and Uxbridge sites—and two more distant groups—Roebuck and Broughton Hill sites in New York. The similarities in the skulls suggest that they came from local populations and probably represented "trophy" heads. Which means they weren't fighting invading strangers—they knew each other.

Iroquoian oral history speaks of this as a particularly brutal time, and clearly the archaeological record supports their stories.

But the violence was also the catalyst for one of the most important events in the history of the world. It led to the rise of a legendary hero, the Peacemaker named Dekanawida, who established the Great Law of Peace and founded the League of the Iroquois—a confederacy of five tribes: the Onondaga, Oneida, Mohawk, Cayuga, and Seneca.

Without the League, the United States would not exist today, nor would our unique understanding of democracy. Concepts like one-person/one-vote or referendum and recall were not European. They were Iroquoian.

And they would prove to be irresistible to the wave of colonists fleeing oppression in Europe.

In 1775, James Adair wrote a book called *History of the American Indian,* in which he described the Iroquoian system of government by saying, "Their whole constitution breathes nothing but liberty...[T]here is equality of condition, manners, and privileges..."

Indeed, the system of government espoused by the League was everything that European monarchies were not. The Iroquois refused to put power in the hands of any single person, lest that power be abused. The League sought to maximize individual freedoms and minimize governmental interference in people's lives. The League taught that a system of government should preserve individual rights while striving to ensure the public welfare; it should reward initiative, champion tolerance, and establish inalienable human rights. They accepted as fact that men and women were equal and respected the diversity of peoples, their religions, economic and political ideals, and their dreams.

Thomas Jefferson wrote, "There is an error into which most of the speculators on government have fallen, and which the well-known state of society of our Indians ought, before now, to have corrected. In their hypothesis of the origin of government, they suppose it to have commenced in the patriarchial or monarchial form...Indian leaders influence them by their character alone...every man, with them, is perfectly free to follow his own inclinations. But if, in doing this, he violates the rights of another...he is punished by the disesteem of society, or...if serious, he is tomahawked as a serious enemy."

On the eve of the American Revolution in 1776, English papers began circulating the following account, which was, incidentally, meant to be insulting: "The darling passion of the American is liberty, and that in its fullest extent; nor is it the original natives only to whom this passion is confined; our colonists sent thither seem to have imbibed the same principles."

Indeed, they had.

Gifted writers like Thomas Jefferson and Benjamin Franklin would openly fan the flames of that "passion" for liberty, and set in motion a chain reaction that has yet to end. That passion would become a sweeping wildfire that would race around the globe and shape the very heart of what would, centuries later, become known as The Free World.

Dekanawida, quite simply, changed the course of history.

We can only imagine the terrifying forces that might have hardened his resolve...

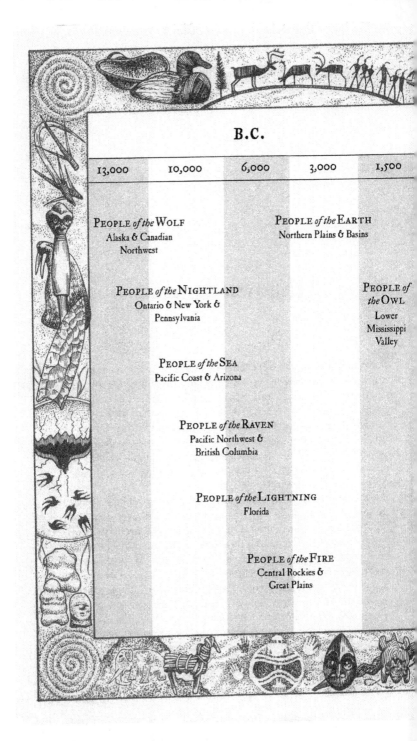

B.C.

13,000	10,000	6,000	3,000	1,500

PEOPLE *of the* WOLF
Alaska & Canadian
Northwest

PEOPLE *of the* EARTH
Northern Plains & Basins

PEOPLE *of the* NIGHTLAND
Ontario & New York &
Pennsylvania

PEOPLE *of
the* OWL
Lower
Mississippi
Valley

PEOPLE *of the* SEA
Pacific Coast & Arizona

PEOPLE *of the* RAVEN
Pacific Northwest &
British Columbia

PEOPLE *of the* LIGHTNING
Florida

PEOPLE *of the* FIRE
Central Rockies &
Great Plains

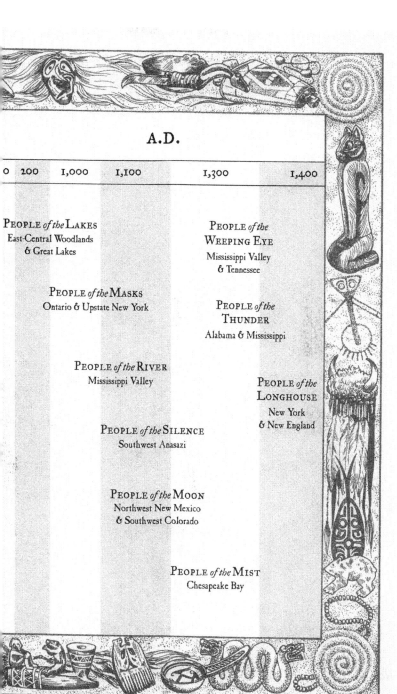

A.D.

| 0 | 200 | 1,000 | 1,100 | 1,300 | 1,400 |

PEOPLE *of the* LAKES
East-Central Woodlands
& Great Lakes

PEOPLE *of the*
WEEPING EYE
Mississippi Valley
& Tennessee

PEOPLE *of the* MASKS
Ontario & Upstate New York

PEOPLE *of the*
THUNDER
Alabama & Mississippi

PEOPLE *of the* RIVER
Mississippi Valley

PEOPLE *of the*
LONGHOUSE
New York
& New England

PEOPLE *of the* SILENCE
Southwest Anasazi

PEOPLE *of the* MOON
Northwest New Mexico
& Southwest Colorado

PEOPLE *of the* MIST
Chesapeake Bay

Skanodario Lake

Canassatego Village

IROQUOIA
The Lands of the
People of the
Longhouse

otarho Village
Yellowtail Village
Bur Oak Village
White Dog Village
Singleleaf Village
Wild River Village

Forks River

Bend River

The Lands of the
People of the
Dawnland

Forks River

Hawk Moth
Village

Singleleaf
Village

Wild River
Village

Bog
Willow
Village

Pine
Hill
Village

IROQUOIA

Rapid River

Quill River

SHADOWED FOREST

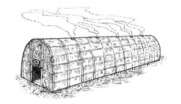

1

"Find anything?" Towa called from the edge of the meadow to Sindak's left.

Tree-covered mountains rolled like storm-heaved waves across the land, rising and falling in breathtaking swaths of autumn color. High above, unmoving Cloud People seemed to be planted in the blue sky.

Sindak lifted his head from where he'd been concentrating on patterns in the frozen leaves. Towa had plaited his long black hair and tucked the braid into the back of his cape. Standing in the snow-frosted grass with two gigantic pines behind him made him seem taller and thinner. As Elder Brother Sun continued his journey to the west, afternoon light streamed between the pine boughs and landed across the meadow like dropped scarves of pure gold.

"No. You?"

Towa shook his head.

Sindak propped his war club on his shoulder and squinted at Koracoo. She was far ahead, walking through a grove of beech trees. He turned around and glimpsed Gonda bent over, searching what appeared to be a rivulet of snow melt.

Sindak called, "I don't understand it. The morning went so well. What happened? Where did we lose it?"

"In that elderberry thicket."

Sindak sighed and propped his hands on his hips. They'd found the trail of the kidnapped children at dawn, and been able to follow it for a full three hands of time; then it had vanished in the middle of an elderberry thicket. It was as though the children had been lifted straight up off the earth and flown away to the Spirits only knew where. Since the thicket, they'd been floundering, going in circles, finding nothing.

Sindak went back to searching. He carefully stepped through the snow-crusted leaves that lined the shadowed west side of the meadow. There was something here, but he wasn't sure what yet. The afternoon warmth had melted out patches of leaves and grass, but he felt certain he was seeing more than that. Here and there, leaves appeared to have been turned over, as though they'd stuck to the bottom of a moccasin and been flipped as the man passed. Unfortunately, the pattern wasn't regular—as a man's steps would be. The enemy warriors were very clever. He stretched his taut back muscles and stared upward. The shadows cast by the branches kept changing as Elder Brother Sun descended toward the western horizon. Each moment, the meadow looked different.

Towa let out a frustrated breath and walked over to Sindak. "I'm starting to feel like we're chasing our tails. As I suggested at noon, we should return to the thicket and start over."

Sindak's bushy eyebrows drew together. "War Chief Koracoo is sure we're on the right trail."

"Yes, but why? We haven't found any sign in over four hands of time."

As they walked, Sindak said, "It's that magical warclub of hers."

Suspiciously, Towa said, "CorpseEye?"

"Yes. It's alive."

Towa laughed disdainfully.

Frozen leaves crackled beneath their moccasins as they walked around a boulder and onto a trail that fringed the trees. Deer tracks cut perfect hearts in the mud. Ahead of them, a rocky granite slope two hundred hands across covered the hillside.

Sindak continued, "Laugh all you want, but you know that trail we were on at dawn? CorpseEye found it."

Towa gave him a skeptical look. "Found it?"

"I know you don't believe it, but I swear upon my Ancestors' graves, it's true. Around midnight we were talking when suddenly Koracoo got a worried expression on her face. When I asked her what was wrong, she said that CorpseEye was old and sometimes he saw or heard things that she did not. When he did, he tried to tell her."

"Her club talks?"

"No...at least I don't think so." Sindak made an uncertain gesture with his hand. "She says the club grows hot, sometimes painfully hot—and that's what happened to her last night. That's why we started searching in the darkness."

Towa stepped over a pile of deer droppings and followed the path as it curved back out into the frosty meadow. Deer trails twined through the fallen leaves, creating a braided weave of shadows, but there was no sign that humans had passed this way. Especially not a war party with an exhausted group of children. Men might carefully follow in each other's tracks to hide their numbers, but children generally failed. They didn't seem to have the ability to concentrate on the task.

"All right. Let's discuss this," Towa said, sounding very logical. "Did CorpseEye actually lead you to the trail?"

"Well, no, not exactly. I found the trail, but—"

"That's what I thought. You're an excellent tracker."

Sindak scratched the back of his neck with his war club. "Maybe, but that pale blue line of stones that we found at the base of the toppled tree? I think CorpseEye led Koracoo to it, and it connected with the trail."

"But the line of stones was natural. It hadn't been placed there by someone. And you told me that you thought the line of stones was in a different place than the blue glimmer you'd seen in the night."

"True, but—"

"Nonsense. It was an accident."

Sindak shrugged. It was generally useless to talk to Towa about supernatural events since he thought they were all wild flights of imagination. "Think what you want, my friend. You didn't touch CorpseEye and feel his Power run up your arm like icy ants."

"Sindak, it's just a very old piece of wood with a red quartzite cobble tied to the top."

"And two black spots for eyes. It watches me, Towa. Really." Sindak stabbed a weed with his war club. No matter what Towa said, he'd *felt* something when he'd touched that club, and he didn't believe in tempting Spirits. "I'm going to do everything I can to make that club like me."

Towa laughed. "You remind me of my cousin."

"Which cousin?"

"The one I despise. Neyot."

"Oh, thanks."

"Neyot once spent three moons trying to make a dog like him, in the hopes that the 'woman of his dreams' would come to agree with her pet."

"Did it work?"

"No. He was always grabbing the animal by the ruff and talking right in its face. The poor, frustrated dog had no choice but to chew off his nose. The incident did not impress the woman of his dreams."

Sindak dredged up memories of Neyot's mangled face. The dog had eaten off the flesh and half the bones. "Your cousin is a dull-wit."

"True. But your wits over the past few days haven't been any too sharp, either. Do you really believe you can seduce Koracoo?"

Sindak tipped his head. "I'm not trying to seduce her. It's just very pleasurable to look at her and dream about her. What's the harm in that?"

"What's the harm? I can't believe you said that. You're going to wake up some night with Gonda's war club embedded in your skull. He may be her former husband, but he still loves her."

"Really? He has a curious way of showing it. All he does is whine and shout at her."

The deer trail wound through the meadow and headed toward the broad granite slope covered with stubby trees. Boulders and broken huge spalls littered the base of the slope. The chances of finding anything up there would be slim. On the other hand, that's exactly where Sindak would have gone if he'd been trying to hide his trail.

Towa massaged his left broken shoulder. While he'd been sleeping with his sling on, he took it off during the day. Walking with his arm hanging straight down obviously caused him pain.

"I don't know why you don't wear your sling during the day, too. It would be easy to throw it aside if we get into a fight."

"If the pain gets too bad, I will." He gave Sindak an askance look. "And you can't change the subject that easily. Every time you talk to Koracoo, I want you to keep the image of a war club embedded in your skull right behind your eyes."

Sindak paused. Finally, he softly said, "I can't help being attracted to her, Towa. What man wouldn't be?"

"Me. But I'm smarter than you."

They walked out of the meadow and into the cold shadows of the boulders beneath the slope. Lichen-covered and streaked with black minerals, many stood four or five times Sindak's height. Every place that a tree could take root, it had; stunted saplings grew in the crevices and curled around the bases of the rocks. In places the saplings grew so thickly, they formed a dark, impenetrable wall.

As Sindak began climbing, still following the deer trail, the earthy fragrance of soaked granite and moss encircled him. In many places, the deer had leaped over the rocks that cluttered the slope. Sindak had to work his way around them while keeping his gaze on the ground, searching for evidence that humans had passed this way.

From behind him, Towa called, "This is going to take time. We have to move slowly through this kind of jumble. I wish—"

"Towa?" Sindak's breath caught. Something sparkled amid the saplings.

"What?" His moccasins grated on stone as he hurried up the slope. "Did you find something?"

Sindak knelt and pushed aside a clump of saplings to reveal the tiny circlet of copper that had lodged in the grass at the base. It was no bigger than a fingernail.

Towa's eyes narrowed. "Don't move. I'll go fetch Koracoo and Gonda."

While Towa trotted away, calling, "Koracoo? Gonda? Come look at this!" Sindak stared at the copper. It was a small ornament with a hole punched in the top. Among the People of the Hills, children's capes or moccasins were often sewn with such decorations. But who knew when it had been lost here?

he could, then sank down on the shore beside them. Long black hair clung to the skulls. He smoothed it away from their gnawed faces to stare into their empty eye sockets. He didn't see them in there, but he hoped the girls' souls were still hovering close by. Soon, he would go searching for them and bring them back to their bodies. Then he would take them to a hilltop and leave their bones facing east, looking in the direction of their Flint families. Perhaps they would recognize the way home, and be able to get there.

He exhaled hard.

Out in the trees, shadows wavered.

A symphony of whimpers, creaks, and birdcalls rode the wind, the music of the forest; it serenaded him as he got to his feet and headed out on his nightly hunt.

3
ODION

Tutelo snuggles against me and whispers, "Brother? Do you see him?" My eyelids flutter, but I do not open them. We marched hard all day. At dark, Gannajero gave us each a single cornmeal biscuit filled with walnuts, the first freshly cooked food we've had, and I was so grateful I gobbled mine down. Right after I brushed the crumbs from my hands and left them in a pile for the birds and mice, I fell asleep. "See what, Tutelo?"

She is being very still, as though trying not to attract the attention of a predator that stands nearby. Her innocent young face with its large eyes and small nose are framed by straight black hair. "Out there, by the fire cherries."

I turn my head to look. There is a big grove of fire cherries twenty paces away. The branches have lost all of their leaves, and in the starlight they look like nothing more than spiky undergrowth. Fog moves along the ground and twines in the canopies of the trees. I don't see anything unusual. Our guards stand ten paces away. The man I call Ugly because of the enormous scar that slashes his face leans against a tree and yawns. His real name is Hanu. He is very tall, maybe eleven hands, and has shoulders like a bear's, broad and meaty. The other guard, Galan, is new. His friend Wrass named him Worm because he is so skinny. Worm has his feet spread and is watching the camp. Gannajero and the rest of her warriors sleep soundly around the fire. While the flames have burned down, the coals blush red when the wind breathes over them. The scent of smoke hangs heavy on the frosty air.

"I don't see anything, Tutelo," I whisper. "Go back to sleep." I roll over.

"No, look, Brother!" she insists, and tugs on my shoulder. "He's right there."

Grudgingly, I roll back over and stare out at the fog. The streamers move like snakes, twining around trunks and slithering over the ground. Beyond the fog, I can make out the dark, looming shapes of sycamores. Their spreading branches reach so high they disappear into the mist. My gaze traces down one massive trunk that is wider across than Ugly is tall. Against the black bark, the elusive wink of starlight flashes on metal.

My breathing dies. I do not blink. Just stare.

It moves, a kind of weightless, leisurely drifting that is as noiseless as the passing of a cloud shadow. For a long while, the only sounds in the night are the soft hissing of the breeze in the trees and the wild hammering of my heart.

Starlight catches in the metal, and there is a prolonged glimmer, as though it has stopped and is watching us.

The hair at the nape of my neck prickles.

Suddenly, a flurry of wings batters the fire cherries, and birds shoot away through the fog. Our guards spin around with their war clubs up, ready to strike down whatever they find. They hiss to each other, study the fog, and Ugly stalks toward the cherries.

Gannajero sits up by the fire and stares out at the fire cherries.

Ugly circles the trees and uses his club to poke between branches. When he is satisfied, he walks back over to Worm and shoves him hard enough to make Worm stagger, then says, "You idiot." They both chuckle, and continue talking softly.

My gaze returns to the fire cherries.

There is something almost hypnotic about the stillness. The wind has stopped. The fog seems to have frozen in place. The dark branches resemble hundreds of fingers reaching toward the Sky World.

A brief blue flicker shines near the big sycamore.

I prop myself up on one elbow. Is it a Forest Spirit?

Odion.

I feel the whisper along my bones, a faint creeping sensation like spiderwebs trailed over the skin.

Terrified, I drag Tutelo against me, shielding her from the unknown. In her ear, I hiss, "Don't move."

She obeys.

Very faintly, I hear it again—the unmistakable sound of my name whispered by a man, and the soft scrape of leather against wood.

Then the trees rustle, and I think I see a dark cape billow as a man walks away through the glistening fog.

Tutelo whispers, "It's Shago-niyoh."

The milky stillness of her calm is unnerving.

"D-did he talk to you?" I stammer.

Tutelo tilts her pretty face and stares at me owlishly. "Did you see him?"

I feel like my lungs are starving. I gasp in cold air before I exhale the words, "I'm not sure. Maybe."

Ugly turns our direction and scowls. "Stop talking. Go to sleep. We have to carry you tomorrow, and it's a lot harder to carry someone who's asleep." He aims his war club at us.

We both stretch out on our sides, and I curl my body around Tutelo to keep her warm. She heaves a weary sigh and closes her eyes.

Blood pulses so powerfully in my veins that I feel slightly ill.

Gannajero rises and silently bird-walks across the ground. Her black eyes are huge and, if I didn't know better, I'd say scared. She stops by her warriors and hisses, "What did you see?"

"Nothing."

"What frightened the birds?"

Ugly shrugs. "I don't know. We didn't find anything."

Gannajero's gaze slowly moves over the fire cherries, as though expecting to see something or someone. No one makes a sound. In the darkness, her greasy twists of graying black hair hang about her wrinkled face like black fringes.

Gannajero takes ten silent, measured steps toward the cherries. She's breathing hard. In a hideous gasp, she says, "It's the *Child.*"

Ugly frowns. "The children are all accounted for. It can't be—"

"He's found us." Gannajero quickly retreats to stand between her warriors. Her gaze darts over the forest, as though an ancient evil has risen and is about to swallow them all.

I twist my head to stare back out at the fire cherries.

Waiting.

But now there is only fog and forest.

Gannajero wildly glares down at me. "Did you call it?"

"Wh-what? I don't under—"

I sit up and her fist is like a meteor plummeting out of the night. It strikes me squarely in the jaw and knocks me hard to the ground. Tutelo screams. I feel dazed. My head is spinning. I can't seem to sit up. All the other children wake and start talking at once, asking each other questions.

"Never call to it!" Gannajero hisses. "Never *speak to* it! Not even if it speaks to you first. Do you understand me?"

I manage to jerk a nod before I roll to my side to spit mouthfuls of blood on the ground. Two teeth roll out. I can feel the gaps in my lower jaw, on the right side.

Gannajero bends over me with blazing eyes. "Tell me you heard me. Don't just nod!"

Before I can speak, she draws back her hand again, and I cover my head, preparing for another blow. But from the corner of my eye, I see Wrass leap up and grab Gannajero's fist as it plunges toward me.

I scream, "No, Wrass, don't!"

Gannajero cries out hoarsely and tries to twist free of his grip. Wrass is hanging on, trying to wrench her arm out of its socket. Her men instantly leap into action. They beat Wrass off Gannajero with their war clubs.

He curls into a ball on the ground, huddling

against the blows. The sound of his grunts and cries wither my soul.

None of us dares go to his aid. We are all too afraid of getting beaten to death ourselves.

"Enough," Gannajero finally orders, and her guards back away.

Wrass is lying with his arms over his head, whimpering, and rolling as though in great pain.

Gannajero meets each of our gazes, and her wrinkled lips pucker as if she wants to spit upon us. "If any of you dares to touch me ever again, you will all be beaten bloody. Do you understand?"

We nod.

Tutelo crawls over to me and puts a cool hand on my back. "Odion? Odion, are you all right?"

"Yes…yes."

Gannajero turns to her warriors. "This means we're being followed. He's leading them right to us. Tomorrow, at first light, I want both of you to scout our back trail. And if you see anything, *anything,* return and tell me immediately."

"Yes, Gannajero."

The old woman marches back to the fire and drags Spirit charms from her pack—painted weasel skins, ancient buffalo horn sheaths, and what appear to be wolf fangs. She places them in a circle around her and begins singing a song that sounds like a series of growls and yips.

Ugly whispers, "What's she doing?"

Worm shakes his head. "I swear she's madder than a foaming-mouth dog."

I crawl over to Wrass. "Wrass? Why did you do that? You should have just let her hit me!"

Wrass is panting and groaning, but he manages to look up at me. Blood coats his entire face like a wash of paint. "We have to protect each other, Odion. No one else is going to protect us."

"But they almost killed you!"

Father was right. Wrass is the warrior. He cannot stand by and watch any of his People hurt.

All of the other children gather around Wrass. Baji is weeping silently, and Hehaka looks like he longs to run away and hide, probably because he knows exactly how Wrass feels. Tutelo has both hands over her mouth, smothering her cries. Only Zateri has the courage to do what's necessary to help Wrass.

"Wrass," Zateri says. "I n-need to touch your head. Is that all right?"

He nods and lowers his hands. The sight almost makes me wretch again. Large patches of Wrass' scalp have been torn loose, revealing the bloody skull beneath. Zateri pulls the scalp back into place and carefully uses her fingers to explore his head, stopping here and there to probe more thoroughly.

"Don't worry," she says to Wrass. "You're going to be all right. They didn't crack your skull, at least not that I can see or feel. But you'll have a bad headache for days." She reaches into her leggings and pulls out a small hide bag. As she loosens the ties, she glances up at the guards. They've returned to talking softly among themselves, smiling. "I gathered these strips of birch bark this morning. Chew on them, Wrass. They will help with the pain." She tucks them in Wrass' hand, but he barely seems to notice. He just shivers and seems to sink into the grass as though he's melting away.

Then Zateri moves closer to me. Her brown eyes are ablaze as she whispers, "I gathered other things today. Special *things*. Skunk cabbage root, spoonwood leaves, thorn apple seeds, musquash roots."

My heart pounds. "Keep them hidden. Tomorrow, we'll figure out what to do with them."

She nods and tucks the small bag back into her leggings. "Odion?" she says, "Wrass needs to be warm. Let's all sleep curled around him tonight."

"Do as she says," I order, as though I am now in charge. Me. The boy who is always afraid.

Zateri is the first to lie down and press her body against Wrass' back. I lie down behind her and reach my arm over Wrass and Zateri, pulling them both close. One by one, the other children join in, pressing tightly together around Wrass, becoming one big, warm animal with many legs and arms.

"Tutelo?" I call.

She is sitting a short distance away, staring out at the fire cherries. Her pretty face is taut with concentration. She must be looking for the Child, the creature she calls Shago-niyoh.

"Tutelo? Are you coming?"

She turns and looks at me. She's sucking on her lower lip, and it makes her face appear misshapen. "He's coming back," she whispers. "I know he is."

I lower my head and rest it on my arm.

I don't know who starts it, but a strange thrum begins. It's like distant thunder, barely heard; then the whispers blend into one low growl as they flash through our group: *"Gannajero says someone is following us. Someone's coming for us. It's my parents! They wouldn't just abandon me! No, our war chief must be searching for us. It's an entire war party. A thousand men!*

Our guards chuckle. They are amused by hope. Perhaps because they've seen it die in the eyes of so many kidnapped children.

I close my eyes and concentrate.

Beneath all the noise, I can hear Father's voice as he jerks me from my bed: "Odion, the village is under attack. Take Tutelo. Run as far away as you can and hide. I'll find you, no matter where you are. *I'll find you."*

Peace fills me. He's coming.

Mother's with him. They'll be here before I wake in the morning. We'll all go home together. We'll help our clan build a new longhouse. We'll be happy…

4

As Gonda slogged through a swampy area on the east side of the pond, hopelessness taunted him. Every time they thought they were on the right path, it vanished. He felt weak and desperate. He didn't know exactly when it had happened, but somewhere in the past few days, he'd lost himself. What remained sickened him—the husk of the strong man he'd once been. And he was weary enough, disheartened enough, that all he wanted to do was to crawl inside that husk and hide forever.

Koracoo met him as he slogged out of the water and stepped onto dry land. She was less than six hands away, and he felt her nearness like a physical blow.

"Did you find any evidence that they marched through the pond?"

He shook his head. His drenched moccasins squished with his movements. "At first, I thought..." He turned to look back across the small pond to the place where he'd thought he'd seen a track. Steep, rocky mountains rose on either side of the narrow valley. Towa and Sindak were still searching the trails that led to the pond. "I didn't even find a bent reed. Did you find anything around the edges?"

Her face was drawn and pale, and the bones beneath her tanned skin were too sharp. Her unevenly chopped hair, cut in mourning for lost loved ones, stuck out oddly from too much time in the wind. "No."

He waited for instructions, but Koracoo just hung her head and closed her eyes, as though too tired to think straight.

"Are you all right?"

"Tired. That's all."

Gonda turned away and looked northward to where a wall of bruised clouds massed.

She had never asked him what had happened the night of the attack. She was a pragmatist. She'd found him, made sure he was all right, and led him back to the burning village to attend the emergency council meeting. The few surviving elders had all blamed Gonda for the debacle. After all, he'd split his forces, disobeying War Chief Koracoo's orders. Yellowtail Village had been overrun almost immediately. Koracoo had carefully questioned each witness, heard their stories, and helped the elders plan what to do next. Then she had walked to the Bear Clan longhouse, pulled out what few belongings she could find that had belonged to him, and set them outside the door—divorcing him.

Less than one hand of time later, they were on the trail, searching for their children. The shame and grief were still unbearable.

"Gonda, I need your advice. What do you think we should do? I'm out of ideas."

He felt a sudden lightness, as though all the horrors that lived inside him had suddenly dropped away. She needed him. He straightened to his full height. "What's CorpseEye telling you?"

She pulled the club off her shoulder and held it in both hands. "He's gone stone-cold."

The two black spots that dotted the red cobble-head of the war club seemed to be looking straight at him, as though to say, *Stop being foolish. You know the way.*

"Perhaps because we're on the right trail," Gonda said.

Koracoo cocked her head doubtfully. "Maybe, but there's so much I don't understand."

"Like what?"

"Why is it that we can track them across bare stone, but not across the ground?"

Softly, Gonda said, "We both know now, don't we? We're not tracking warriors with slaves.

Warriors heading home wouldn't take the time to hide their trail this way."

She jerked a nod. "We both know."

Hesitantly, he continued, "There's something I've been thinking about."

"What?"

The sudden arrival of a flock of crows made her look up. The black birds cawed as they playfully dove and soared, their ebony wings flashing in the sunlight.

"I have the feeling we're tracking an orb weaver, Koracoo."

"An orb weaver?" They were spiders that spun spiraling webs.

"Yes. Each night the spider's old web is replaced by a new one, spun in complete darkness by touch alone."

"You mean she travels at night?"

"I mean she's a creature of darkness. She stands in her web at night, but retreats from it during the day. I suspect that all of her spiderlings do the same. She orders her warriors to meet in a certain place at nightfall, but at dawn—"

"They scatter."

Tingling heat flushed his body at the look on her face. She stepped closer to stare him in the eyes. "During the day, they all take different paths to hide their numbers? That would explain some things. It is much easier to track a war party than a single man, especially a skilled warrior taking pains to hide his trail."

"They could each be carrying a child. If that's what they're doing, we need a new strategy."

The longer they stood staring at each other, the more powerfully he longed to touch her. Strands of black hair curled over her tanned cheeks, and there was something about the sternness of her expression—as though she were holding herself together by sheer willpower—that built a desperate need in his heart.

"What are you thinking?" Gonda asked.

"I'm wondering if Towa wasn't right to begin with. We should spread out more. Work exactly the opposite of how we've been working. Instead of walking eastward, paralleling what we think is the trail, perhaps we should work perpendicular, cut across the forest from north to south looking for a sign."

Emotion rose up to choke him. She was right. Why hadn't he thought of it himself? Gonda lifted a hand to touch her face, but halted, and let it hover awkwardly. If she would only take a step toward him. But she did not, and he clenched his hand into a fist and lowered it to his side.

"Let's try it," he said simply. "It's a good idea."

She held his gaze for far longer than she had since the attack. It was an instant of shared hope and pain, and he cherished it. He engraved her expression on his soul, so that he could pull it up again and again when he thought he could bear no more of the futility of the search.

"Koracoo, I wish that you and I..." Tears burned his eyes.

He clenched his jaw and looked away. She hated excessive emotion. She said it weakened everyone around him. He recalled once on a raid when a man had thrown himself over the body of his dead friend and begun wailing. The grief had spread like a contagion. Within ten heartbeats, every warrior was sobbing or sniffling. Koracoo's response had been to walk straight to the man who'd started it and slap him senseless. Shocked, he'd looked up at her. She'd ordered, "Get up now, or you'll be joining your friend in the afterlife."

Gonda blinked away his tears and shot a look at Towa and Sindak. They were carefully examining the bark on an oak tree, as though they'd found something. For the past hand of time, they'd been walking through gigantic oaks. A canopy of laced branches roofed the trails and cast brilliant geometric patterns across the acorn-covered ground.

"All right," he said. "Here's my advice: If we don't find anything here, I think we should split up, send Towa and Sindak back to the place where we lost the trail, and let them cut for a sign while you and I continue north and do the same thing."

"When and where will we meet?"

"What about dusk south of Hawk Moth Village? You know the place where the main trail forks?"

They both watched Sindak. He'd climbed up into the oak and seemed to be examining the limbs. Below him, Towa was apparently asking questions —his mouth was moving.

"It's risky. We'll be on the border of Flint People lands. They might kill us just for daring to step into their country."

"We were worried about the same thing with Atotarho. We survived. The Flint People could have been attacked, as well, and be searching for missing children. Maybe we could help each other."

Wind blew her short hair around her face, spiking it up more than before. She faintly resembled a startled porcupine. In the old days, he would have told her that, and she'd have laughed. But there was no laughter between them now.

"All right. Let's tell our allies the new plan." Koracoo started back for Towa and Sindak.

Gonda followed her around the edge of the pond and back into the laced shadows cast by the heavy oak boughs. Even the small limbs were as wide across as his shoulders. These ancient giants must have seen hundreds of summers pass.

Sindak jumped down from the tree, and he and

Towa watched their approach with narrowed eyes. Towa stood a head taller than Sindak. He'd braided and coiled his long hair into a bun, then pinned it at the back of his head with a rabbit-bone skewer. The style made his handsome oval face appear regal. Sindak, on the other hand, looked shaggy. His shoulder-length hair was disheveled and matted to his forehead by sweat. In the mottled light, his deeply sunken brown eyes resembled dark pits, and his hooked nose cast a shadow.

"War Chief," Sindak said. "We found something."

Koracoo picked up her pace. "Show me."

All four of them gathered around the base of the oak, and Sindak put his finger below a fresh scar on the bark. It was a lighter-colored patch, no bigger than a thumb.

Gonda examined it and said, "It might be a scar left by a buck. They sharpen and clean their antlers on the trees—but it's small for an antler rub."

"Or it could have been made by a flicker. They love to bury insects in cracks in the bark," Koracoo added.

"That's what we thought at first," Sindak said. He shoved damp hair away from his homely face and continued, "But if you look at the rest of the tree, you'll see more of them."

Sindak climbed back up into the tree, and Gonda followed him. As they climbed higher, the rich fragrance of wet wood encircled them. Gonda breathed it in—a soothing scent that reminded him of his childhood, when he'd done a great deal of tree climbing.

Sindak stepped out onto the first major branch and bent down to show Gonda another bark scar. This one was even smaller than the first, but clearer. "If you climb higher, you'll find these small scars on almost every branch."

Gonda stared upward into the crooked sunlit limbs. A few old leaves and acorns clung to the highest branches. They swayed in the breeze. "Are the scars always right next to the trunk?"

"Yes."

Sindak was looking at him expectantly, as though the truth should be obvious.

"So," Gonda said, "you think someone climbed up here using the limbs as a ladder?"

Sindak pointed to the place twenty hands above them where the massive limbs of two trees met. "Right there, where the limbs overlap, it looks like the climber stepped from this tree to the next one.

"And if you'll look over there," he pointed to a place where the limbs of the next tree overlapped with a tree farther north, "you'll see that he could have moved to yet another tree."

Gonda let his gaze scan the oaks. With careful planning, a man could go a long way climbing from one tree to the next. And if he did it often, he could do it relatively quickly.

"They...they're climbing through the trees? Is that why we keep losing the trail?"

Sindak nodded. "It might be. I have noticed that every time we lose it, we are surrounded by giant hickories, or oaks, or other big trees with spreading limbs. That's what made me start looking closely at the trunks. I wanted to see if I could spot scars left by feet."

Hope flooded Gonda's veins, and without thinking, he slapped Sindak on the shoulder approvingly. "You are a good tracker, Sindak. Just the way Towa said. Let's tell the others."

They climbed down.

Before they'd even jumped to the ground, Koracoo called, "Well? What did you find?"

Gonda said, "Sindak is right. There are scars all the way up the trunk. Someone has been using the trees, climbing through the branches, moving from tree to tree."

"We can't be certain, of course," Sindak said, "that this is the trail we seek, but it's a trail."

Koracoo's gaze shot upward and darted over the limbs, moving, as the climbers must have, from one heavy limb to another to another. It would have been even easier for children. They were lighter and could have used more of the forest canopy to travel. "This changes everything."

"What do you mean?"

Gonda nodded at her, then said to Towa, "Earlier, Koracoo and I were talking. Koracoo said that instead of paralleling the trails, we should cut across them, moving from north to south, searching for signs. But now that we know they are using the trees—"

Towa interrupted. "Wait. Are you suggesting that the warriors are...are each walking different trails? That's why you want to cut for a sign from north to south?"

"We think it's possible."

Sindak rubbed a hand over his face as though stunned by the realization. "Of course they are. That's how they do it. If each warrior takes one or two children and picks his own route, he can climb over rocks, wade rivers or ponds, and climb through the trees. That's why the sign is so confusing."

Towa seemed to be putting all the pieces together, and not liking what he saw. His expression became a grimace. "If this is true, their trails may be spread out over a vast area of forest. It's going to take forever—"

"That's why no one has ever been able to track Gannajero." Koracoo was gazing out into the depths of the forest, but thoughts moved behind her dark eyes. "Time. The trails seem to go in different directions. They start and stop, or vanish altogether. It takes so much time to unravel them that people give up."

"If only we had another fifty warriors," Towa said, "we might be able to do it. But without them? I don't know."

Frustration was building. Gonda could feel it in the air. The task suddenly seemed overwhelming. Despair lined Towa's young face, and Sindak looked angry.

Gonda said, "We don't need fifty warriors."

"Why not?" Towa raised his voice. "How can four people accomplish anything? I—"

"Listen to Gonda," Koracoo said. She was watching Gonda, waiting to see what he was doing before she interfered. It was the way they'd always operated. They worked as a team to get their warriors to figure out the problem.

Gonda continued, "You were right in the beginning, Towa. We need to spread out so that we can cover more territory. We'll arrange a place to meet at night; then, over supper, we'll discuss what each of us has found, and pick which trail to pursue the next morning. We'll follow it until it disappears. When it does, we'll return to cutting north-south again."

"It seems like we're grasping for—"

"Towa." Koracoo put a hand on his shoulder, and he turned to peer into the dark depths of her eyes. He looked faintly mesmerized. "Think this through. If you were arranging such a ruse, how would you do it?"

Towa shook his head as though he had no idea, but after a few moments, he blinked, and said, "Well, I—I suppose I'd tell my warriors to fan out—to get as far from each other as they could—and to pick the most difficult paths through the forest. Both strategies would slow the pursuers down to a crawl and give me more time to get away."

"But..." A thoughtful expression lined Sindak's beaked face. "As the day wears on, as each person gets closer to the meeting place, the trails will start to converge."

"Yes." Gonda nodded. "And that's the first thing we should look for. Patterns like that. If we can figure out even the most basic pattern, it will cut our search time in half."

Koracoo gazed up into the oak tree to study the interlacing branches again. Sunlight sheathed every twig. "If we assume that this is one of the trails, and they are headed east, there should be other trails to the north and south of this one. We just have to find them."

Cloud People drifted through the sky high above, and their shadows roamed the trees like silent Spirits, plunging them into a suddenly dimmer world. Wind murmured through the branches, rising and falling in an ominous cadence. Gonda waited until the shadows had passed, and

Elder Brother Sun's gleam again sparkled through the trees.

"All right," Gonda said. "Where are we going to meet?"

Koracoo answered, "The main trail forks just south of Hawk Moth Village. I say we meet there."

Gonda turned to Sindak and Towa. "Do you know where that is?"

"Yes," Sindak said. "We've been there several times, on raids. Frankly, I don't think the Flint People like us very much. If they catch us, they're liable to cut us into tiny pieces and feed us to their dogs."

"The same is true for us. That means we need to stay out of their way," Gonda said.

Koracoo gestured to the oak tree. "Sindak, you found the scars on the tree. Why don't you start with this trail?"

"Yes, War Chief." Sindak grabbed a branch and started climbing up into the oak.

While she watched him, Koracoo said, "The rest of us will spread out along an east-west line and start walking north, cutting for a sign. I'll start from here—the base of this tree."

Gonda looked at Towa. The youth still had a skeptical, disheartened expression. "Towa, I'm going to trot east for two hundred paces, then cut north. Why don't you trot west for two hundred paces, and cut north? If you find a sign, follow it out. If not, don't worry about it—just meet us at dusk south of Hawk Moth Village."

Towa nodded. "I'll be there." He took off at a slow trot, heading west.

Gonda headed east. When he turned to look over his shoulder, he saw Koracoo walking due north into the jade-colored pines, and Sindak maneuvering through the bare oak branches, tracking his prey from tree to tree like an overgrown squirrel.

5

The pattering of acorns falling on the forest floor mixed with the pounding of Towa's heart. Somewhere close by he heard movement. It might be an animal, but he was fairly certain it was a man.

Gently, so he made no sound, he grasped the scrub oak branch blocking his path and eased forward. When he'd stepped by, he returned the branch to its former position and scanned the deep forest shadows. Slippery elms and yellow birches were in the process of crowding out the oaks. As he tiptoed by a birch, he silently broke off a twig and chewed it. The flavor of mint filled his mouth. Birds watched him, their feathers fluffed out for warmth, but few dared to chirp. He lifted his nose and sniffed the air. A curious odor rode the breeze, like days-old blood, and he thought...

"Sondakwa?" a man called in a strained voice. "S-Sondakwa! Where are you?" Brush crashed and twigs snapped, as though he'd stumbled.

Towa nocked an arrow in his bow and forced a swallow down his dry throat. The wind gusted, and a wealth of acorns let loose. When they struck the brown leaf mat, they made a faint drumlike cadence.

More stumbling...then a voice: *"Sondakwa? Is that you?"*

Something swayed ahead. Towa stood perfectly still, watching. The man thrashed through the brush, panting and whimpering. He had a war club in his fist.

Towa drew back his bowstring, just in case, and his shoulder wound ached with fiery intensity.

"Sondakwa, where are you? Stop hiding from me!"

As he came closer, Towa could see the man better. He was big, stocky. Black geometric tattoos covered his face. To create the designs, warriors pricked their flesh with bone awls, then rubbed the tattoos with charcoal to darken them. The sides of his head had been shaved in the manner of the Flint People, leaving a central roach of hair on top. A few limp, soaked feathers decorated the style.

The man staggered and had to grab hold of a birch limb to keep standing. Then he lifted his head, saw Towa, and pinned him with wide, vacant eyes.

Towa blinked. The impact of that gaze struck him like a spectral fist in the dark. His scalp prickled. When his grandfather had been dying, there had been a moment at the very end when Grandfather's eyes had suddenly opened...but there was no soul there, no awareness, just a sort of surprised stare. That's what he saw now.

Softly, Towa called, "Who are you?"

The man didn't seem to hear him. He kept holding onto the branch for a few instants longer. Then he swayed on his feet, and slowly toppled facefirst to the ground.

Towa watched him for fifty heartbeats before he released the tension on his bowstring and gazed out at the trees again. Only a few faint triangles of sunlight managed to pierce the canopy. The rest of the forest was cloaked in shadow. The man had been calling to a friend. Was there someone else out there Towa needed to worry about? He inhaled a breath and let the scent of wet wood fill him, then cautiously walked forward.

Towa stopped two paces away and studied the man's shaven head and the white feathers in his roach. The man didn't seem to be breathing. His war club had bounced from his hand, but it was within easy reach.

Towa slung his bow and tucked his arrow back

into his quiver; then he pulled his war club from his belt.

Leaves crackled as he walked to stand over the man. He kicked him in the side. Nothing.

Towa knelt and scooped leaves away from the man's face. His brown eyes were open, and dead. But just to make sure, Towa touched the man's eyeball with his finger. Again...nothing. Towa flipped the man's cape up and tugged his pack from his shoulders, then rummaged through it.

Stunned, he pulled out a magnificently etched copper breastplate. Leather cords hung from the corners of the plate, clearly for tying it on. A master artisan had etched the copper with hundreds of miniature False Faces. Some had wide smiling mouths and long noses. Others had hideous, terrifying expressions with enormous eyes.

Towa rested it to the side and continued going through the pack. The breastplate seemed to be the only thing of real value the man owned—along with several bags of food.

"You won't need these anymore," he said softly as he drew open the laces of several small sacks that contained jerked duck, hard acorn meal biscuits, sunflower seeds, walnuts, and hulled beans. Even a bag of what looked like chunks of dried squash.

Towa stuffed all the food into his own pack, then rose to his feet. He didn't know what to do with the copper breastplate. It was too large to carry in his pack. But he certainly wasn't going to leave something so rare and beautiful here to corrode. It was awkward with his wounded shoulder, but he managed to flip up his cape and tie the breastplate over his chest.

Towa squinted at the man's trail. He could see it clearly in the leaves. It was serpentine, weaving all over the place. He followed it eastward.

Late in the afternoon, Towa reached up, taking sight of the sun and moving his hand, palm width by palm width, to the western horizon. He had less than one hand of time left before he'd have to head straight for the fork in the trail to meet Sindak, Gonda, and Koracoo. He continued following the dead man's trail.

When he entered a thicket of shining willow, he saw two deep knee prints, then another set, and nearby he found grooves in the mud left by frantic fingers. The man had fallen down several times in the thicket, clawed his way back up, and staggered on. Towa kept walking. On the other side, he saw a narrow deer trail lined by holly and headed for it, expecting to see more of the man's tracks there.

Instead, he found another set of tracks. The man's lost friend?

Towa knelt to examine them. The distinctive herringbone weave was made only among the Hills People. He whispered, "A Hills warrior? What are you doing out here, my friend?"

As he rose to his feet, he wondered if one of the other Hills villages had dispatched a war party into Flint lands. If so, this man had gotten separated from his party, because there was only one set of prints.

Or...perhaps Chief Atotarho, his own chief, had decided he couldn't trust Koracoo and Gonda? Atotarho had ordered Sindak and Towa to accompany War Chief Koracoo to help find the chief's missing daughter, Zateri.

Towa's thoughts drifted back to his conversation with Koracoo the first night on the trail, when she'd suggested that Atotarho had not sent Towa and Sindak to help rescue the girl, because he'd wanted his daughter to be captured. That idea had been plaguing Towa for days. His hand rose to touch the sacred gorget where it rested beneath his cape. Atotarho had given Towa specific instructions to present the gorget to Gannajero within moments of laying eyes upon her.

But he did not know why. The gorget was valuable, yes, very valuable, but would it be enough to buy back Zateri and the other children?

Towa didn't know.

He backtracked the herringbone trail until it intersected with the dead man's tracks, and his eyes narrowed. Something strange had happened here. The dead man had started running, first in one direction, then another, charging about as though being pursued. But the herringbone sandals hadn't moved. He'd been standing still.

A cold shiver climbed Towa's spine.

"Why did you start running? Did you see something that frightened you? Why didn't the man wearing the sandals run?"

Wind clattered in the branches—a thin rattling that reminded Towa of teeth chattering.

He ran his fingers over the copper breastplate beneath his cape and tried to fathom what had happened here. The dead man had been panicked, taking long strides; he'd clearly been running for his life.

Towa turned to stare at the herringbone sandal prints again...and decided to follow them.

Twenty paces later, he stumbled over a second dead man. Another Flint warrior, or at least he wore the same hairstyle. The first man's lost friend? Sondakwa? Towa walked closer. He saw no blood. The man hadn't been shot, or clubbed; he just lay sprawled on his back, staring emptily up at the storm clouds that filled the afternoon sky. He looked like he'd just fallen down dead on the trail.

Towa glanced around. Birds and squirrels hopped through the trees, unconcerned, but a deep, gnawing sense of dread filled him.

"I have the feeling," he whispered uneasily as he stared at the herringbone sandal prints, "that now I know what frightened the first man into running. I wish I had more time to track you, my Hills friend."

But he didn't.

Towa checked the faint shadows, figured the direction, and broke into a trot, heading for the rendezvous place.

6

Rain fell, misty and cold, from a charcoal-colored dusk sky. Sindak's cape and war shirt dripped onto his moccasins as he maneuvered around the hickory trunk, trying to remain hidden. He felt like a hunted animal, running for its life with no hope of escape.

Soft steps pattered the trail behind him. At first, he'd thought the sounds were nothing more than splashes of rain hitting the ground, until one of his pursuers stepped on a twig and snapped it. Now he knew better. The stealth with which they stalked him told him they were warriors.

How many?

Doesn't matter. Even if only one man is following me, he might be the advance scout for an entire war party.

Sindak looked northward. White pines covered the hilltop where he'd taken refuge, but in the distance he could see giant hickories and beech trees thrusting up through the ground mist. He was less than a half-hand of time from the fork in the trail where he was supposed to meet Towa, Koracoo, and Gonda. It was too late to make a mad dash for them, and he wouldn't even if he could. No matter what happened, he would not lead the enemy to his friends.

As the steps came closer, he heard murmuring. One voice? Two? He couldn't be sure. Sindak nervously licked his lips. There wasn't enough light left to effectively use his bow. If they came at him, he'd have no choice but to start swinging his club and pray.

More murmuring, the voice at once sad and reproving, as if the man were speaking to a wayward child.

Sindak closed his eyes to hear better, and it magnified the shishing of the rain and the faint tapping of the man's feet on the trail.

More than one man...

The steps of the other two people were almost inaudible. More like wings batting air than moccasins striking earth.

It was almost night. Surely these warriors would return home when they could no longer see.

Sindak didn't move a muscle, but his gaze drifted northward again.

Towa would just be starting to worry. He'd be staring out into the darkness with a frown on his face, probably cursing Sindak for being late. In another hand of time, Towa would stop cursing. No matter what War Chief Koracoo said, he would trot out into the forest to start looking for Sindak, and maybe run right into the arms of Sindak's pursuers. Sindak couldn't let that happen.

He sniffed the rain-scented breeze. It was pine-sharp and cold. Wherever men went, they carried with them the odors of their fires or their sweat, maybe the food they'd spilled on their capes. He didn't smell any of those things.

In the distance, silver light penetrated the storm clouds and shot leaden streaks across the pine-whiskered mountains. Here and there, orange halos of firelight painted the underbellies of the clouds, marking the locations of villages. The glow to the east was probably Hawk Moth Village, but it could be a large war camp. In all likelihood, the men who followed him were from there; warriors sent out to scout the Flint borders.

Very faintly, a voice called, *"Odion?"* Then, again, *"Odion?"*

Sindak's breathing went shallow.

The howls of hunting wolves echoed through the trees as the steps moved, almost silently, up the trail less than fifty paces away. Then he heard a strange rattle. Branches clattering together in the breeze? An odor he knew only too well wafted to him: the stink of rotting flesh.

A shiver climbed Sindak's spine.

To make matters worse, there was only one set of footsteps now. Where were the others? Had they split up? Maybe they'd spotted him and two of the warriors were sneaking around through the trees, hoping to surprise him.

Frantically, he searched every place a warrior might appear. The storm light made the brush and rocks look like crouching beasts. He gripped his war club in both hands.

The steps moved past him, heading up the trail with catlike grace. Barely there. Just one man, but clearly a man who had lived too long with death to ever be careless.

The man's cape slurred softly over the ground, and Sindak thought he heard weeping—but it might have been the wind through the branches.

Sindak waited for the rest of the war party he was certain would be coming.

The whisper of the man's steps eventually died away.

Sindak boldly chanced looking around the tree, out into the twilit stillness where rain sheeted from the sky and created shining puddles in every hollow. He saw no warriors.

After another quarter-hand of time, Sindak risked stepping from behind the hickory. Darkness had taken hold of the world. He flipped up the hood of his cape, quietly walked out onto the trail, and ran north toward Hawk Moth Village as fast as his legs would carry him.

While they waited, Gonda, Koracoo, and Towa gathered pine poles and created a makeshift ramada beneath a birch. Covered with a mixture of pine boughs and moss, it was mostly dry underneath.

"Where is Sindak?" Gonda grumbled as he crawled under the ramada and sat down cross-legged.

"I'm sure he's coming." Miserable and wet to the bone, Koracoo sat in the rear, hunched over a cup of rainwater. This close to Hawk Moth Village, they couldn't light a fire for warmth or cook food for fear that they'd be seen.

Gonda said, "I say we forget about him and go to sleep."

"Let's give him a little longer." Koracoo leaned back against the birch trunk.

"He's irresponsible," Gonda said. "He should have been here two hands of time ago."

As soon as he'd said the word *irresponsible,* brief, agonizing images of Yellowtail Village flitted across Koracoo's souls. She forced them away. How strange that she felt nothing now—nothing except a weariness that weighted her limbs like granite and a hunger that made her knees tremble. Even her anger was gone, replaced by a lassitude in which all things seemed vaguely unreal.

She stared out at the growing darkness.

"Something must have happened," Towa replied from her left, where he stood against the shelter pole. "He wouldn't be late unless something had happened."

"You'd better be right. If he wanders in here with no wounds, I'm liable to give him some," Gonda replied.

Towa's mouth quirked, but he obviously knew better than to say anything. He glanced unhappily at Koracoo, who just shook her head lightly and looked away. From the corner of her eyes, she studied Gonda. He restlessly twisted his cup in his hands. His hair and clothing were soaked, and he looked to be on the verge of an enraged fit. Rage was his way of dealing with fear. Perhaps it was the way every warrior dealt with fear, but she pitied him. She had never pitied him before. He had always been the strength in her heart, and the warmth in her souls. When had he become so weak and frightened? She wondered if maybe Sindak hadn't been right after all, that she shouldn't have brought him along.

No, despite everything, he deserves to search for his own children, to know for certain that he's done all he can to find them. I owe him at least that much.

Gonda took a sip of water and glared out at the rain.

Koracoo refilled her cup from a thin stream that ran off the roof and took a long drink. When Sindak arrived, if he arrived, they would discuss what each person had found and make their decisions about what to do tomorrow. The rain was going to make things much harder for them. They needed a good plan and as much rest as they could get.

Towa picked up one of the brown twigs that littered the ground and toyed with it, tapping it on his palm. "Maybe he found the trail. Did you think of that? Maybe Sindak found it and followed it for as long as he could before he lost the light."

"I hope so. That's the only thing that will save him from my wrath." Gonda tugged his hood down over his forehead and clutched it beneath his chin. "Since none of us found anything significant today, what are we going to do tomorrow?" he asked belligerently.

Koracoo said, "Towa found fifty tracks, and two

dead men, and I found two clumps of rabbit fur on branches."

"The dead men probably had nothing to do with our children, and two clumps of rabbit fur? That's nothing. It could have been left by—"

"I've never seen a rabbit jump ten hands high," she said before he could finish his tirade. "Therefore, I assume they were ripped from a cape. I consider both finds to be significant."

"So are you saying I'm the only one who found nothing?"

She almost shouted at him, but stopped herself. Images fluttered up again, and she saw Yellowtail Village burning, filled with smoke, dead bodies laid out like firewood. Her children gone. Her husband missing. It had been the worst she could imagine. Running through the flaming longhouses, searching for survivors, the screams of the dying, hands plucking at her cape. And when she thought it could get no worse, she'd found her mother and sister burned almost beyond recognition.

The eyes of Gonda's souls must be seeing things equally as bad, or worse, since he'd fought the battle. Guilt was smothering him—but she could not waste the strength to care.

"Our plan worked, Gonda." Koracoo shifted to bring up her knees and propped her elbows atop them. Her red cape looked black in the storm light.

"Both trails appear to parallel the route Sindak found through the trees this morning."

"Both trails? They weren't trails. At best, they were—"

"They were trails." She bent over and drew three short lines in the wet dirt, showing the approximate locations of the sign they'd found. The lines were staggered. Towa's trail was far west of Sindak's, and Koracoo's trail was far east.

"It takes a good imagination to see those three dots as parallel trails, my former wife."

For just an instant, utter despair tormented her. She longed to yell that it was because of him that she would never again lie down as a mother and wife with her family's love surrounding her. She would never again be able to look across the longhouse where she was born and gaze into her mother's wise old eyes, or watch her sister cooking supper. Small things. Things she'd taken for granted now meant everything to her.

When grief began to constrict the back of her throat, she said harshly, "They are trails. If you can't see it, it's a good thing you're not in charge."

The words must have affected him like lance thrusts to his heart. His mouth trembled. He shouted, "You mean, *as I was at Yellowtail Village?*"

"Be quiet, you..." She bit back the bitter words and forced herself to take a deep breath.

Towa was watching them with his eyes squinted, as though considering whether or not to run before Koracoo and Gonda brought the entire Flint nation down upon them.

"We're just—we are all exhausted and hungry," Koracoo said. "Let's not argue."

Gonda glowered down into his cup. Black hair stuck to his cheeks, making his round face look starkly triangular. His eyes resembled bottomless holes in the world.

Towa cautiously reached out and tapped the ground beneath the dots. "All three trails seem to head in the same direction, almost due east, toward the tribal home of the People of the Dawnland. I agree that it may be coincidence, but—"

"Even if they do all head east, it means nothing! We didn't find a single track today made by a child. Your 'trails' could have been made at different times by different war parties, scouts, or hunters that have absolutely nothing to do with our lost children!" Gonda declared.

Towa drew back his hand and tucked it beneath his cape. "Yes. True."

On the verge of hopeless fury, Gonda set his cup aside and stared up at the roof.

Calmly, Koracoo said, "We need to focus on the task. If we—"

Feet pounded the trail to the south. Each of them reached for weapons and turned to look at the windblown pines. The trail, which ran with water, shone as though coated with molten silver.

"Move," Koracoo said as she pulled CorpseEye from her belt, got to her feet, and slipped out into the rain behind the tree. Gonda and Towa vanished into the mist.

As the Cloud People shifted, a distant flicker of starlight glinted from the eyes of a man on the trail and illuminated a pale face. Koracoo studied him. She hadn't known Sindak long enough to memorize his movements, but she thought it was him. The wind stirred the hem of his cape, swaying it. As he trotted out of the trees and saw the fork in the trail, he grew more careless. His long stride quickened, and his feet splashed in the puddles.

Thirty paces away, Towa stepped from where he'd been hiding in a copse of dogwoods, and Sindak broke into a run. Towa trotted out to meet him. They embraced each other, and a hushed conversation broke out as they headed back toward the ramada.

Koracoo remained hidden behind the tree. The pines whispered in the wind, but she thought she heard something else out there. A voice...or distant music. Singing?

Gonda ducked beneath the ramada again and slumped down in his former position. As the two young warriors trotted up, his eyes narrowed. He looked at them like they were the enemy. Which, they were, until recently.

Sindak and Towa crawled beneath the ramada, smiling, glad to see each other, and Towa said, "See, I told you he was coming. Where's Koracoo?"

"What took you so long?" Gonda asked.

Sindak unslung his bow and quiver and set them in the rear of the shelter; then he sank to the ground and heaved a sigh. "I was followed," he said. "I had to hide while the warriors passed by."

"Followed? Did they see you?"

"No." Sindak shook his head, and his shoulder-length black hair flung water droplets in every direction.

"How many were there?"

"Three, I think. I was afraid to look when they passed by, but it sounded like the steps of three people."

Towa dipped his own cup beneath the water stream coming off the roof and handed it to Sindak. "Here. You must be thirsty."

Sindak took it with a grateful smile. "I am. Thanks." He emptied the cup in four deep swallows and handed it back to Towa. "Where's Koracoo? I have news."

Koracoo silently stepped from behind the tree and walked back toward the ramada. The rain had lessened a little. Stars glimmered in the distance.

When she got to within five paces, she softly called, "What news?"

Sindak swiveled around to look at her. "I found a trail, War Chief. A clear trail. It was made by three people. They kept climbing into the trees, traveled for a ways, then climbed down and walked on the ground before they retreated to the trees again."

Gonda said, "It was probably an earlier trail made by the same three people who followed you."

Sindak sat back at Gonda's harsh tone. "I suppose it might have been."

Koracoo knelt just inside the ramada. Towa and Sindak turned to watch her with expectant eyes. Koracoo reached over to the place where she'd drawn the fragments of trail earlier. "This is where your trail started this morning." She tapped the place. "Show me the one you found today. How did it run? Where did you lose it?"

Sindak bent over the drawing and carefully sketched out what he'd found.

Towa glanced up at her. "Sindak's trail runs parallel to the one you found, Koracoo."

"Yes. It seems so." She squinted at it.

Sindak frowned before asking, "These other lines are trails? You also found trails?"

"We think—"

Gonda interrupted. "Don't be fools. We've lost the trail completely, and we all know it!"

Koracoo didn't even deign to glance at him. She looked at Sindak. "How far east of here did your trail end?"

"About a half-hand of time. But I—I didn't lose it, War Chief. I was still on it when I realized I was being followed and had to hide. After that, it was too dark to search any longer, so I ran directly here."

Koracoo nodded. "You did excellent work today, Sindak. And you, also, Towa. We know a good deal more tonight than we did last night. Tomorrow, we will all fan out and try to follow Sindak's trail. It seems to be the clearest. We—"

"This is a waste of time!" Gonda snarled.

"*I* decide when it's a waste of time, Gonda. Not you."

He flopped onto his side and turned his back to them.

Towa and Sindak went silent. They both stared questioningly at Koracoo. She said, "I will take first watch tonight. The rest of you should get some sleep."

As she rose to her feet, grabbed CorpseEye, and stepped out into the light rain, she heard Sindak ask, "What did you find today, Towa?"

"Two dead Flint warriors, and—"

"What killed them? Certainly not two arrows from your bow. You've never hit two targets in a row in your life."

"See? This is why it's hard to imagine some-times that you're my best friend."

"Of course I am. So, someone other than you killed them. Who?"

Towa made an airy gesture with his hand. "They may have been killed by a Hills warrior. I'm not sure, but I found about fifty tracks made by a Hills warrior near both of the bodies."

"Really? How do you know he was one of our People?"

"His sandals had our distinctive herringbone weave—"

A cold tingle climbed Koracoo's spine. She whirled around at exactly the same instant that Gonda lurched to sit up. He had a panicked expression on his face. Drenched black hair stuck to his cheeks.

Towa's voice died in his throat. He blinked at them. "What's wrong?"

Gonda said, "Was he a—a big man? Did his tracks sink deeply into the mud?"

"Yes, that's why it was easy to track him...at least for a short distance."

Koracoo held Gonda's gaze. "It may be just another Hills warrior."

"Wearing sandals in the winter? I doubt it. He's following us."

As though a dark, cold feeling was forcing him

to stand, Towa got up. "Who? Who is following us?"

Koracoo walked back and stepped beneath the ramada to face him. Towa stared at her like a suspicious animal. "The morning after the attack," she explained, "Gonda found a similar track. Made by a big man wearing sandals with a distinctive herringbone weave."

"Where?" Sindak asked.

"Far south of here," she said. "Near Canassatego Village."

"Canassatego Village? That's Hills country. What were you doing there?"

"We were tracking the warriors who attacked our village and captured our children."

Towa stood for a moment, not certain what to say. "I thought you said Mountain warriors attacked Yellowtail Village?"

"Most were." Gonda drew up his knees. "I'm not sure they all were."

In the long silence that followed, Koracoo heard a dog bark in the distance, and then the faint shout of a man. Both came from the direction of Hawk Moth Village. The sculpted curves of Towa's face hardened as he clenched his jaw. For a time, she watched the thoughts churning behind his dark eyes and thought he might stalk away. Finally he said, "Where did the big man's tracks lead?"

Gonda answered, "You know that enormous shell midden—"

"The one that sits on the border between our countries?"

"Yes. The man's tracks led to the top of the midden."

Towa shifted his weight to his other foot. "Why? What was he doing up there?"

"Carrying a body. A dead girl. And one of high status, too, given her jewelry."

Astonished, Sindak said, "She was still wearing jewelry?"

"Yes. Strange, isn't it? Any warrior worth his weapons would have stripped every piece and taken it home with him."

Towa asked, "Why are you telling us this? Do you think the girl was one of Gannajero's captives?"

"No. Gannajero is a Trader. Her warriors would definitely have taken the girl's beautiful copper earspools and shell bracelets. And her shell gorget with the magnificent False Face surrounded by stars—"

"She was wearing a False Face pendant?" Towa asked as though shocked. "With stars?"

Gonda created a circle with his fingers and lowered it to his chest to show them the size. "Yes. A big one. And the False Face had a serpent's eyes and buffalo horns..." He stopped when both Towa and Sindak went rigid. They looked like surprised geese. "What's the matter?"

Koracoo studied them as they whispered to each other. Towa had placed a hand over his heart, as though protecting something hidden beneath his cape.

"Is that Atotarho's gorget you're touching?" she said.

As the storm drifted eastward, starlight broke through the clouds and brightened the night. The rain-slick ground shone with a frosty radiance. Every twig and branch seemed to be coated with a thin layer of silver.

Koracoo said, "Why don't you show it to us, Towa?"

Towa carefully pulled a huge gorget from his shirt and let it rest upon his cape. It covered half his chest.

Gonda leaped to his feet and extended his hand. "Let me see that?"

"No," Towa said. "He ordered me to wear this at all times. It's been in his clan for hundreds of generations. It's been passed down from matron to matron since the creation of the world."

"But it's identical to the one we found at the midden," Gonda charged.

Towa shrugged. "There are supposed to be two. Don't you know our story of the battle between Horned Serpent and Thunder?"

Koracoo leaned her shoulder against the ramada pole, and the wet hem of her cape stuck to her leggings. "It's very similar to our story, isn't it? At the dawn of creation, the Horned Serpent attacked People, and the Great Spirit sent Thunder to help humans. In the battle that ensued, Thunder threw the greatest lightning bolt ever seen. The mountains shook, and the stars broke loose from the skies. One landed right on top of Horned Serpent."

Towa continued, "Yes. This pendant chronicles that sacred story."

Koracoo stared at the gorget that rested like a shining beacon on Towa's cape. The carving was exceptional. The stars shooting around the head of Horned Serpent seemed to be coming right at her.

"Why have you kept it hidden from us?" Gonda asked.

"Because it's not a thing for ordinary eyes, especially not Standing Stone people eyes. It's ancient. Can't you feel its Power?"

"I can," Sindak said, and backed away. "It gives me a stomachache."

A stray breath of wind stirred Koracoo's hair, and she jumped as if at the touch of a hand. "Why would the dead girl have had an identical pendant?"

"It couldn't have been identical," Towa said. "It must have been a fake, a copy."

Gonda shook his head. "I don't think so. It was exactly like the one you're wearing."

Towa shook his head vehemently. "It can't be."

"Why?"

"Because the other belongs to the human False Face who will don a cape of white clouds and ride the winds of destruction across the face of the world. Obviously a dead girl can't do that." Towa stuffed the magnificent gorget back into his shirt. "It was a fake."

Gonda's gaze flitted to where his pack rested, as though he longed to go get it, but he didn't.

Koracoo waited for a time longer, then said, "The end of the world will, I suspect, take care of itself. In the meantime, you suggested that the Hills warrior with the sandals might be following us. Why?"

Gonda's brow furrowed. "He may just be tracking the children like we are, and so his path necessarily intersects ours."

Koracoo said, "Towa? Sindak? Your thoughts?"

Towa scanned the darkness. "He is a Hills man, that's certain, but—"

"Unless he stole the sandals." Sindak folded his arms across his chest. "He could have taken them during an attack on a Hills village— which means he could be a Flint warrior, or Landing warrior, or anything else. Even a Standing Stone warrior."

Koracoo gently smoothed her fingers over

CorpseEye while she considered his words. The polished wood felt like silk. He was right. The sandals told them nothing certain about the man— if it was the same man. But...if he had followed them, there was a reason. Was he a spy for Atotarho? Keeping track of them? If so, the man would have been dispatched with several other warriors—runners he could send home to keep the chief informed of their progress, or lack thereof. If he was not one of Atotarho's spies, Gonda could be correct that he was just a desperate family member trying to track down his own captured children, and his path happened to coincide with theirs. In that case, he might be an ally, at least in this pursuit —as Towa and Sindak were.

It was the last possibility that made her hands clench tightly around CorpseEye. The sandaled man could be a scout sent out by Gannajero to monitor her back trail to see if she was being followed. If so, right now, he could be running ahead to tell the old witch about them.

"It's getting late. Let's all think about this, and we'll discuss it more tomorrow. Gonda, I will wake you at midnight."

He nodded.

Koracoo walked out into the starlight and took up her guard position beneath a towering oak tree. In the dark rain-scented gloom, three deer trotted by, their pale antlers swaying in the ashen gleam.

She watched them until they caught her scent and disappeared into the trees like silent ghosts.

The three men beneath the ramada stretched out and pulled their capes around them for warmth. It took less than a few hundred heart beats for Sindak to start snoring softly. Gonda, lying close beside him, seemed to be staring up at the ramada roof. Towa had his back turned to both of them.

After a time, Koracoo's thoughts returned to the gorget.

If the pendants were not identical, they were very nearly so. The only way an artist could have accomplished such a feat was if he'd been holding Atotarho's pendant in his hand when he'd carved the second one.

And that led her to some wild speculation. What if—

Movement caught her eye. She straightened suddenly. It resembled a black spider, far out in the darkness, silently floating between the trees, paralleling the trail that headed north. Now and then starlight reflected from its body, revealing long legs and perhaps flashing eyes.

It's probably just another deer.

But tomorrow at dawn, she would check for tracks to make certain. It kept her alert and watching every wind-touched limb that swayed... while she contemplated the possibility that the sandaled man had given the dead girl the pendant to take with her to the afterlife. Even if it was a superlative fake, it would have been a rare, precious gift. Why? Had she been a relative? Or was he trying to buy her goodwill? Perhaps to help him when he reached the bridge to the afterlife?

On the other hand, maybe he'd given it to her so that she could take it to the human False Face in the Sky World and set him on his journey, fulfilling the prophecy.

Koracoo knelt at the base of the oak and wondered.

8

Dim bluish light filtered through gaps in the ramada's roof and landed like a finely woven scarf across Gonda's face. He rolled uncomfortably to his side and struggled to get back to sleep. Sometime during the night, Sindak and Towa had rolled closer to him, pinning him in. He could barely stretch his legs out. Worse, the constant low drone of the wind slashed through his dreams, becoming Tawi's voice every time he drifted off.

After an eternity of restless shifting, he finally rolled to his hands and knees and crawled over near the tree trunk, where he stretched out in the soft, sweet-smelling birch leaves and closed his eyes again.

Sweat drenched his face; it rolled down his neck to soak the collar of his hide shirt. He wiped his forehead on his sleeve and stared blankly at the patchwork patterns of light that decorated his closed eyelids. Weariness clung to his shoulders like a granite cape.

Gonda! Tawi screamed.

"Stop it," he whispered. "Stop dreaming. You can't change it."

Moments later, he felt himself sinking deeper into sleep. His breathing melted into soothing rhythms. The sounds of the wind faded. Darkness smothered the light...

And the snow fell around him in huge wet flakes. "Where, Tawi?"

"Over there!" Her voice wavered in the icy gusts that lanced Yellowtail Village. Tawi pointed. "Near the giant oaks!"

Tawi looked so much like her sister, Koracoo, that sometimes it stopped Gonda in his tracks. She was beautiful, with an oval face and large dark eyes. Though tonight, fear twisted her features.

Gonda ran along the palisade catwalk, confidently slapping warriors on the shoulders as he passed, trying to get closer to the place Tawi swore she had seen movement in the forest. She ran behind him, her moccasins patting softly on the wood.

Warriors had been coming to him for over a hand of time, whispering that they'd seen movement out in the trees, reporting vast numbers of enemy warriors sneaking through the darkness. But there'd been no attack. No warriors had materialized. Everyone was so terrified that he wasn't sure who or what to believe.

"When will Koracoo be back?" Tawi asked as they continued along the catwalk. "I thought she was supposed to be here before dusk."

"She was. I'm worried about her."

Gonda was more than worried. He was terrified that something had happened. Had she met the full force of the enemy out there? Was she even now fighting a desperate retreating action, trying to get back to the safety of Yellowtail Village? Or worse? Had she and her scouting party been ambushed and destroyed? He longed to dispatch a war party to go look for her, but she had ordered him to keep all of his three hundred warriors inside the palisade until she returned. It seemed foolish. If he could just send out five or six scouts, they might be able to bring him enough information about the enemy's strength that he could prepare for the attack he felt sure was coming.

But he would not disobey her orders. He never had.

Besides, she'd dispatched two scouts at dawn. Neither had returned.

Tawi grabbed his shoulder hard. "Right there. See?"

She pointed, and Gonda stared out into the darkness.

"There, Gonda! In the center of the oaks."

Gonda pulled an arrow from his quiver and nocked his bow while he scanned the trees. "Tawi, all I see is falling snow and branches blowing in the wind. What did you think you saw?"

"It wasn't just me, Gonda. Four of us were standing here when we saw flashes in the oaks."

"Flashes?"

"Yes, like chert arrow points winking. Or maybe shell beads."

Gonda squinted at the oaks again. On occasion, as a limb flailed, the old autumn leaves flashed silver in the starlight that penetrated the clouds.

"There's something out there, Gonda. I swear it."

"I believe you, Tawi. I just don't see it." He turned and looked out at Yellowtail Village. Three longhouses encircled the plaza, one for each clan: Turtle, Bear, and Wolf. Unlike the Hills or Flint Peoples, they had small longhouses, barely two hundred hands long, but each stood over thirty hands tall. The elm-bark walls looked shaggy in the snow. The plaza was dark and empty, but the fire-light seeping between gaps in the longhouse walls cast a pale amber glow over the forty-hand-tall palisade of upright pine poles. There was only way into the village—the massive front gates. He'd stationed fifty warriors inside to guard the gates. The rest of his warriors were on the catwalk, staring out at the darkness. He could hear them hissing to each other, and the fear in their voices made his stomach muscles knot. "Is the village prepared?"

"Yes, all of the children are in bed being watched by elders."

"Good. I—"

"Gonda!" a woman shouted.

He spun and saw young Kiya, fifteen summers old, waving her bow at him. "Two runners! Coming from the west!"

Gonda sprinted toward Kiya and gazed out over the chest-high palisade wall. They'd just stepped out of the forest. One man was supporting the other. Both looked wounded. "It's Coter and Hagnon. Quickly, climb down. Tell our men to open the gates."

As Kiya ran to obey, Gonda tucked his arrow in his quiver, slung his bow, and trotted down the palisade, repeating, "We're going to open the gates. Prepare to be stormed. Keep your bows focused on the area just in front of the gates! We're going to open the gates. Get your bows up! Be ready! This could be a ruse to get us to open the gates! Don't be fooled!"

As he raced for a ladder and began to scramble down, his nerves were strung as tight as a rawhide drum. He hit the ground running.

Just before he arrived, two warriors pulled the gates open barely the width of four hands, and the scouts slid through. "Close the gate!" he shouted. "Get the planks down!"

Men dropped the locking planks back into position, securing the gates.

Inside the village, noise rose, people asking questions, running along the palisade to look down at the wounded scouts, arrows clattering in quivers.

But outside...outside...Gonda heard nothing.

He lunged for Hagnon, who had Coter's arm draped over his shoulder. "Marten? Take Coter to one of the medicine elders. See that he's taken care of, then get right back here!"

"Yes, Gonda."

Marten pulled Coter's arm over his own shoulders and started dragging him toward the closest longhouse.

Hagnon looked like he was about to collapse. Streaks of blood covered his square-jawed face and splotched his war shirt. "Gonda, G-Gonda, I—"

"What happened? Tell me quickly."

With terror-bright eyes, Hagnon grabbed Gonda by the shoulders and leaned forward to hiss, "They let us through, Gonda. They thought it was a big joke."

"Who did?"

Hagnon shook his head. "Most are Mountain People warriors, but there may be Hills or Landing warriors out there, too. There are so many, I didn't—"

Gonda grabbed his arms and shook him. "How many? Quickly!"

Hagnon swallowed hard and glanced at the nearby warriors. Softly he replied, "There must be, I—I don't know, maybe over one thousand, Gonda. Or...more. I—I didn't get a good look. They are spread out through the forest, aligned for waves of attacks."

Gonda felt like he'd been kicked in the belly. He released Hagnon's arms, stiffened his spine, and praised, "You are worth your weight in copper, my friend. Your bravery will be rewarded. Now get to the Wolf Clan longhouse and tell the matrons what we're facing."

"Yes, Gonda." Hagnon tried to trot away, but ended up staggering.

When Gonda looked back he found himself surrounded by warriors. All eyes fixed on him, waiting for the bad news. In the faint firelight cast by the houses, their faces looked pale and drawn.

Gonda held out his hands and made a calming motion. "Now, remember, no one has ever breached these walls. So long as you each do your duty, we'll make it through this. Do you understand? Just do your duty."

"But, Gonda..." Kiya wet her lips and stared at him with huge eyes. "Did he say over a thousand?"

"Hagnon couldn't see very well, Kiya. He was wounded, scared, trying to protect his friend; he probably saw far more warriors than there were. I'm sure I would have."

A small round of nervous laughter went through the crowd.

Gonda smiled and raised his voice for all to hear: "And it doesn't matter how many there are! You are well trained. I've seen to it myself. I know you can fight off any attack. You're the finest warriors in the land! Now, get to your posts!"

Warriors scattered.

Before Gonda had taken two steps, war cries tore the air and the people on the catwalk started shouting and running. The enemy hit the palisade like a hurricane, shaking the ground at his feet...

Gonda woke. He glimpsed branches above him and heard rain falling. The colors melted together as images collided and spun wildly, carrying him back to...

The plaza throbbed with a sourceless pounding of sobs and angry shouts. Women moved among the wounded who had been dragged against the southern palisade wall behind the Wolf longhouse. They yelled to each other to make themselves heard over the roar of battle. Orphaned children huddled together between the longhouses, crying and reaching pleadingly for anyone who passed by, calling the names of family members who would never answer again. Scents of urine mixed nauseatingly with the coppery odor of blood.

"Blessed gods," Hagnon murmured darkly. "How many have we lost?"

"Too many," Gonda answered. "I need to know what the matrons think. Has Chief Yellowtail given any orders?"

"I can tell you what the matrons think; they say we must keep fighting. And Chief Yellowtail is too injured to say anything. I'm not sure he's going to make it through this. Is there any hope that the surrounding Standing Stone villages may be sending warriors to our aid?"

"None. That's why our enemies attacked at night. No one will see the smoke from the fires until dawn."

"Gonda, everyone is asking the same question." Hagnon lifted his arms. "Where's Koracoo and her war party?"

A sinking feeling invaded Gonda's belly. He

balanced on a knife's edge, waiting for the moment when he would know all was lost, and he had to give the order to run. "I don't know, Hagnon. I—I don't know."

He couldn't let himself think about her, or he'd crumble into a thousand pieces. At least their children were safe in the Bear Clan longhouse, warm in their hides, being watched over by Koracoo's mother, Jigonsaseh.

He ran a hand through his drenched black hair. What was going on out there? It was like the enemy was holding back, waiting for something. They kept attacking in short bursts, shooting arrows at the warriors on the catwalk while others ran up to the palisade with pots of oil and tossed them on the walls. The last wave would line up outside the trees and shoot flaming arrows into the oil and over the walls into the longhouses—or anyone who happened to be standing in the open.

"So far, we've been lucky," Hagnon said. "We've been able to put out all the fires they've started."

"The snow has helped. Things are too wet to burn easily."

Those with the worst injuries had been laid out side by side in the middle of the plaza. There was no hope for them. If they happened to be struck by an arrow, it would be a quick way to die. Moans penetrated the melee. Gonda followed a winding path that led around them and looked upon the wounds with a horrified feeling of despair. Many had belly wounds. Others had heads or chests bandaged with blood-soaked rags. Most were dying, dying swiftly, their strength too drained by the loss of blood to survive.

Gonda trotted down the length of the house, past the five central fires, to where the clan matrons huddled together. Standing beside the gray-haired elders was the Speaker for the Women, Yanesh, who announced the matrons' decisions.

When Yanesh saw him, she rushed to meet him. Tall and thin, with long, graying black hair, she had a dignity about her.

"Yanesh, have they heard my reports? Have they met in council? What are they saying?"

She took him by the arm and led him away. "They met with the council less than a half-hand of time ago. They say we must keep fighting. They say Koracoo is coming."

Gonda rubbed a hand over his numb face. It felt like an act of betrayal to say it, but he whispered, "I'm not sure she is, Yanesh. Something's wrong, or she would have been here by now. The time is coming, soon, when they will have to decide what to do if the enemy breaches the palisade."

"They have already decided, Gonda. We will keep fighting."

A weary fury seared Gonda's veins. "No. No,

they don't understand. We should plan some kind of diversion that will allow the women and children to escape. Maybe if we can lure the enemy out into the forest—"

"We will keep fighting, Gonda. We will fight until Koracoo arrives. Elder Wida had a vision that Koracoo will arrive at the last instant and save us."

Gonda stared at her. Though he believed that unseen Spirits walked the land, and that souls traveled the Road of Light in the sky to reach the afterlife, he'd never put much faith in visions. "Yanesh, please. Tell them what I said. *Make them understand!*"

Yanesh put a comforting hand on his shoulder. "I will Gonda. Now, you'd better return."

Screams rose outside, and a series of thuds sounded on the longhouse roof. Within moments, flames burst to life.

"Bring the ladders and water pots!" Yanesh shouted.

As people scurried to obey, Gonda sprinted out into the plaza. Hundreds of flaming arrows arched through the night sky overhead, leaving smoky trails. He ran hard for the ladders that led up to the catwalk and climbed swiftly to look out over the palisade. As he unslung his bow and pulled an arrow from his quiver, a strange hush settled over the enemy.

Gonda frowned. He was standing next to Kiya. "What are they doing?"

"I don't know," she said. "After they fired the flaming arrows, they all retreated into the trees and went silent."

"Silent? Why?"

"Maybe"—she wet her lips—"'maybe they're leaving. Maybe they've decided the cost is too high. We've killed hundreds of their warriors."

Gonda surveyed the dead bodies that scattered the area between the gates and trees. He guessed the number at around two hundred— not nearly enough to make them quit, though many had also been wounded and dragged off.

His gaze lifted to the trees. As though a monster had awakened, thousands of eyes suddenly sparkled in the light of the fires. They were on the move. Winding through the trees. Their grotesque shadows wavered against the stark fire-dyed forest.

"They...they're moving their forces up." He spun around and shouted, "They're coming! Get ready!"

Though he heard a few whimpers eddy down the line, his warriors stood tall, their nocked bows aimed at the tree line.

When the enemy finally emerged from the shadows, Gonda stood stunned.

They'd been reinforced. They'd kept him busy

while they'd assembled the necessary forces for one massive final assault against the palisade.

The enemy war chief, a tall man wearing a wolfhide headdress with the ears pricked and the long, bushy tail hanging down his back, strode out front and raised both hands high into the air, as though daring anyone to shoot him.

"Blessed Spirits, that's Yenda." Gonda's belly muscles clenched tight. The last time they'd fought, it had been a chance meeting of two war parties in the forest. Gonda and Koracoo had barely escaped with their lives. The man was the most powerful and revered Mountain People war chief in the land. He was also a filthy murderer. Gonda pulled his bowstring back and held it taut.

"Yenda? Are you sure?" Kiya asked.

"I'm sure."

"Gonda!" Yenda roared like an enraged bear and spread his muscular arms wider. "You see, I brought friends this time. Prepare to die!"

Gonda shouted back, "After you, Yenda!" and loosed his arrow. The white chert point glittered as it sailed down. Yenda spun just in time. Gonda's arrow lanced through his cape.

"Attack!" Yenda shouted, and waved his warriors forward.

They burst from the trees like ants swarming from a kicked anthill, and hundreds of arrows streaked through the starlight. "Fire!" Gonda shouted, and spun to...

He jerked awake, panting, his heart hammering his ribs.

Koracoo turned from where she stood beneath the oak, watching the trails. His eyes locked on her, and he thanked the Spirits that she was alive. *She's alive. Everything is all right.*

But as the memories of the final outcome flooded back, he weakly rolled to his side and gazed out across the rolling starlit hills.

The entire world seemed to be dying around him, and he didn't know how to stop it.

9
ODION

To the east, a turquoise band stretches across the horizon, but the arching dome of Brother Sky still glitters with the largest campfires of the dead. The leafless hickory trees to the north resemble a gray haze, spotted here and there with evergreens. Soft voices carry. Gannajero and her men stand around talking. They have already packed up. We'll be going soon.

We children sit in a circle, waiting for orders. Zateri has her arm over Wrass, who lies curled on his side. He's been throwing up all morning. His face is a mass of swollen purple bruises. If I didn't know it was Wrass, I'm not sure I'd recognize him.

Tutelo and Baji kneel to my left. Baji's gaze keeps searching the clearing, as though she expects to see her relatives appear at any moment. Or perhaps, like me, there's a war party woven into the fabric of her souls. Right behind her eyes. A war party erupting from the trees with bows aimed, killing Gannajero and her men.

Soon...please, Spirits...

This morning, hope is like a wild, starving beast in my heart, eating me alive.

The short, burly warrior, Waswan, tramps away from Gannajero and calls, "Here, you brats. Biscuits!"

When he gets closer, he tosses us each an acorn-meal biscuit.

With a sense of panic, I watch mine arc through the air. It takes forever to fall into my hand. By the time I catch it, my stomach is twisting and squealing. I immediately bite into it. It tastes stale, but wonderful. In no time, it's gone. I lick the crumbs from my hands and stare down painfully at the tiny bits that remain. Leaving anything for the hungry birds and mice is becoming almost impossible.

I hesitate. I can't seem to force myself to brush the bits onto the ground. Grandmother always said if you took care of the animals, they would take care of you. Our People believe that animals allow themselves to be killed. They see a human's hunger and willingly sacrifice themselves so that the One Great Life of all might continue. Every time I brush the crumbs from my hands, I am, in a small way, sacrificing for them.

The other children are breathlessly watching me. They seem to be waiting to see what I do.

I clamp my jaws. My hands are shaking when I brush the last bits of biscuit onto the ground.

They do the same.

Zateri has the harder problem. She is holding Wrass' uneaten biscuit.

"Wrass?" she says softly. "You should try to eat."

"No, I—I can't. Please save the biscuit for me." He keeps his eyes closed, as though the pale beams of dawn light slanting through the trees are stilettos puncturing his brain.

I'm not sure, if I'd been holding the biscuit, that I could have saved it for him. But Zateri is braver than I. She tucks it into the top of Wrass' leggings and says, "It's there when you want it, Wrass."

"Thank you," he answers weakly. "I know th-that wasn't easy." He slits open one badly swollen eye and smiles gratefully at her.

Zateri's face brightens. She strokes his hair gently. "Try to sleep for as long as you can."

Tenshu and Waswan stand talking five paces away. Tenshu is thin, with a deeply lined face and sunken cheeks. Waswan's is glaring at him. His square jaw moves with grinding yellow teeth. He's knotted his greasy black hair at the base of his skull and secured it with a shell comb. He wears a new cape today, made of finely smoked elk hide. Across the bottom, there are white images of wolves chasing each other. He must have won it in the last game.

They both turn to watch Gannajero and Kotin. The

old woman's gravelly voice is too low to hear, but she's waving her arms, and I wonder what has upset her.

Tenshu says, "Gods, what's wrong with her? We're headed to our biggest game ever. She should be leaping with joy."

Waswan's moonish face twitches. "All morning long she's been ranting about the Child."

Tenshu shakes his head. "There was no child. Hanu and Galan both searched the fire cherries. She's lost her soul, Waswan. Maybe we should get out of here before she kills us."

"One more game; then we'll go."

Tenshu massages the back of his neck. "All right. I just wish she'd let us travel the rivers. It would be so much faster. I hate these steep mountain trails."

"And she hates the waterways. There are too many people. Rivers are crowded with towns, people fishing, and canoes. She's afraid someone might recognize her."

"Well, it slows us down."

Zateri glances at the guards, then leans forward to whisper to me. "Tonight. We have to do it tonight."

I jerk a nod and mouth the word: *Tonight.*

Kotin steps away from Gannajero and calls, "Waswan? We'll meet at the Quill River camp north of Bog Willow Village. Don't be late! We're expecting hundreds. Get going."

The short, burly warrior says, "Yes, Kotin," and turns to me. "You, boy. You're coming with me today."

I stand up. "But, please, what about my friend, Wrass? He's too sick to walk all clay."

Waswan says, "He'll either walk, or he'll die on the trail with his head split open. Now, move. This morning, we're starting off in the trees. Go to the hickories."

I turn to wave good-bye to Tutelo, who watches me walk away with wide, frightened eyes.

Tenshu walks up to the rest of the group and says, "You two girls are coming with me." He points his war club at Tutelo and Baji.

They both stand.

I lose sight of them as I march out into the forest with Ugly. Wrass and Zateri must both be going with Kotin, because Gannajero always travels alone. Once we part at dawn, none of us see her again until dusk.

"That one." Waswan aims his war club at the high-spreading branches of the largest hickory. In the sky above, Cloud People drift, their bellies glowing pale gold. "Climb up."

I grab hold of a low limb, brace my moccasin on the hickory trunk, and pull myself up.

Waswan climbs behind me. When I reach the first large limb, I take a moment to grind my heel into the bark, then lift my nose to smell the air. A frightening scent rides the wind. I twist around on the limb to scan the brightening horizon. There is a black splotch…

"Hurry up, boy! You're slow today."

"Do you smell that?" I sniff the east wind.

"I told you to climb. Do it!" He pulls a stiletto from his belt and stabs the bottom of my moccasin. The sharp tip goes straight through the hide and punctures my heel.

"I'm going!" I say. Tears burn my eyes as I climb higher. I finally step out onto the thick limb that leads to the next tree and begin working my way across it. I pretend I'm balancing on a log bridge across a creek.

Father's voice echoes in my ears: *Just watch your feet. Don't look down.*

Halfway across, I grab hold of a branch that sticks up, and turn back to look at Waswan. He has stopped.

He's standing on the limb with his hands propped on his hips, staring out at the narrow valley that cuts through the mountains. A black cloud of smoke trails across the sky. The acrid scent of burning longhouses grows stronger as we climb.

"What village is that?" I ask in a trembling voice. The burning village lies where the valley runs down to a wide river, perhaps a half-day's walk away.

Waswan's head doesn't move, but his gaze lowers to me, and hatred gleams in his eyes. I do not know why he hates me, but he does. Perhaps because I am a Standing Stone boy.

"That's Bog Willow Village. It's one of the filthy villages of the Dawnland People. By now, they're all dead or run off."

"Who attacked them?"

"Men that you will meet tonight."

"How do you know? D-did your people attack the village?"

He stares straight through me as though I'm not really here. "Keep moving, boy. We have a long way to go." A cruel smile twists his mouth. "And tonight is your night. Many victorious warriors will be there."

I'm shaking as I edge out onto the limb and hurry across it. *Don't think about it. Don't imagine...*don't.

Runners often come to speak with Gannajero in the middle of the night. They wake me, but they never stay for long, and they always leave with a bag of riches. I have wondered what they tell her. Perhaps they are warriors about to attack a village? Does that mean there will be new children joining us tonight?

I climb onto the giant limb of the next tree and head for the trunk. When I get there, I wrap my arms around it and rest my cheek against the cold bark while I grind my heel again. My whole body suddenly feels like it's roasting. I can't think straight.

Waswan crosses behind me and orders, "Climb down. We'll walk through the rocks for a time; then we'll climb up again."

I place my feet on the branches like a ladder's rungs. Just before I jump to the ground, a squirrel chitters and leaps away through the tree. While I'm watching, Waswan nocks an arrow and shoots it through the heart. The squirrel falls as lightly as a feather. It makes a soft thud when it strikes the earth.

I jump to the ground, and Waswan climbs down beside me. Without a word, he walks over, pulls his arrow from the squirrel, and tucks the small dead animal into his belt. Its bushy tail glints reddish in the fading light.

"Walk," Waswan orders. "Straight toward Bog Willow Village."

"But it's burning. Why would we go there?"

He gestures toward the rock outcrop ahead. "Stop talking, boy. Walk."

10

As Sindak led the way back to the place where he'd hidden the night before, icy leaves crunched beneath his moccasins. He felt vaguely numb. He hadn't gotten much sleep in the last three nights, and that, along with the fact that they hadn't been eating well, was taking a toll on his strength. He veered off the trail and headed out into the glistening grass. Frost coated everything this morning, shining like a thick layer of crushed shells in the tawny halo of morning light that lanced through the trees. The brittle mustiness of late autumn filled the air.

"Where are we going?" Koracoo called from behind.

Sindak pointed with his bow. "Over there. See that huge hickory tree? That's where I hid from the warriors last night."

Towa's distinctive steps were close behind him. Koracoo was slightly farther back, and Gonda's footsteps came from far in the rear. Sindak turned halfway around to look back. Gonda was trudging along with his head down, as though totally defeated. His war club was almost dragging the ground, and he didn't even seem to notice.

Towa caught his gaze, turned to look back at Gonda, and trotted forward to catch up with Sindak. In a low voice, he said, "I think he's becoming a liability to us."

"He is. But until Koracoo figures that out and orders him to go home, there's nothing we can do."

Towa's buckskin cape fluttered around his long legs as he walked at Sindak's side. "Even if Koracoo ordered him to leave, I doubt he'd do it."

"I suspect you're right. He's going to stick to us like boiled pine pitch until he gets us all killed."

Sindak followed his own tracks across the frozen mud toward the leafless hickory. "Did Gonda keep you awake half the night with his moaning and thrashing?"

"Yes. I was deeply grateful when Koracoo woke him to take his watch. That's when I finally got to sleep."

Sindak sighed. "Me, too."

As they approached the hickory, the cold indigo shadows of the massive limbs began to enfold them. Sindak tugged his cape more tightly around him, and circled to the left. His own tracks were unmistakable. Last night's mud had squished up around his moccasins, leaving clear prints that, this morning, were crusted with frost.

Sindak stopped and waited for Koracoo, and eventually Gonda, to arrive.

Sunlight tipped Koracoo's lashes with gold as she looked at him. Even exhausted, trail-worn, and filthy, she was still a beautiful woman. Her large dark eyes resembled black moons, and the dawn light blushed color into her small nose and full lips.

In an irritated voice, Gonda said, "Did you plan on showing us something, Sindak?"

"What? Oh... yes." He turned, embarrassed. Had he been staring at Koracoo? "This is where I hid last night to allow the warriors to pass by."

"And where were the warriors?"

Sindak gestured out toward the trail that forked thirty paces away. Towering pines scalloped the edges of the path. "The warriors came up the trail and took the fork that heads off to the west."

Gonda shoved black hair out of his eyes before he stalked over to examine the trail.

Koracoo said, "Where did you leave the children's tracks?"

Sindak swung around. "Right back there, War Chief. In that grove of chestnuts."

Koracoo's gaze traveled up the trunk of the

closest tree and into the branches that stretched almost two hundred hands in the air.

On one of the largest limbs, a squirrel sat chewing a chestnut. Discarded bits of the nut fell from its jaws and floated down like brown snowflakes to litter the ground at the base of the tree.

"Koracoo?" Gonda called. He was kneeling in the frosty trail, outlining something with his fingers.

She turned and frowned. "What did you find?"

Gonda waved her over. "Come and see for yourself."

"He must have found the trail of the warriors who chased me last night," Sindak said, and trotted toward Gonda.

Sindak and Towa arrived a few steps ahead of Koracoo, and the three of them bent over Gonda, trying to see what he'd discovered.

Gonda tipped his chin up to look at Sindak. "I thought you said there were three warriors? I only see the tracks of one man."

Sindak's bushy brows pulled together over his hooked nose. "I heard the footsteps of three people," he insisted. "At least for a time. Then two vanished, and only one remained." He straightened and looked behind him, to the south. A mixture of pines and birches gleamed in the sunlight. "Perhaps the other two veered off back there somewhere."

Gonda grumbled under his breath, and Koracoo said, "Gonda? See if you can find any other tracks in that direction."

Gonda rose to his feet and started walking back along the trail, searching. Sindak turned to go with him, but Koracoo said, "No, stay here, Sindak. Help me follow out these prints. Towa, why don't you go and help Gonda."

Towa's mouth pursed distastefully, but he said, "Yes, War Chief," and trotted away.

Koracoo watched him go with narrowed eyes. When he was out of earshot, Koracoo looked at Sindak. "What do you see down there in that track, Sindak?"

Sindak knelt to examine it more carefully. In places the frost had created a strange pattern of tiny intersecting bars. It almost looked...""Blessed Spirits," he whispered. "That's a herringbone design! You don't think—"

"I'm not sure what to think." Koracoo swung CorpseEye up and propped the club on her left shoulder. The breeze blew her short hair around her face. "I wanted to get your impression before I brought it up with the others. Did he sound like a big man when he passed you last night?"

Sindak thought about it. "It was raining, War

Chief. The wind was blowing through the trees. There was a lot of noise. I can't say for certain."

She watched him through hard, unblinking eyes. "What else did you notice?"

He flapped his arms against his sides. "Not much. As I said, for a time I thought I heard three people's steps, then two vanished...and at one point I would have sworn I smelled rotting flesh."

Koracoo cocked her head. "Rotting flesh?"

"Yes, the tang reminded me of a three-day-old battlefield."

Koracoo rubbed her thumb over CorpseEye. "Anything else?"

He thought about it. "I heard a rattle, like branches clattering together in the breeze. And, off and on, I heard the man speaking to someone. I couldn't make out any of his words, but he sounded sad. At one point, I thought he called—"

"Koracoo?" Gonda leaped to his feet and trotted back toward them carrying something.

"What is it?"

Gonda lifted the scrap of cloth into the air, holding it high enough for her to see. "It's a fragment of a girl's dress, I think."

Koracoo's face suddenly turned to stone, and Sindak wondered if she feared it might be from her daughter's dress, as the copper circlet had been.

Koracoo wet her lips, seemed to gird herself,

and walked out to meet Gonda. "Let me see it." She held out her hand.

Gonda draped the soft doe-hide over her palm. Red-and-yellow quillwork decorated the lower half. "It isn't from Tutelo's dress; don't worry about that," Gonda said, alleviating her fear immediately.

As relief shot through her, she seemed to deflate like an air-filled bladder. The hide in her hand quaked softly before she clenched her fist around it. "The quillwork is exquisite," she remarked; then she lifted the fragment and smelled it. "Is this what you smelled last night, Sindak?" She held it out.

Sindak leaned close enough to get a good whiff of the putrid odor. "Yes. But the taint on this fragment is faint. I could not have smelled this from thirty paces away behind the hickory tree."

"No," Koracoo replied softly, and turned the fragment of dress in her hand to study the quillwork. As though something horrifying had occurred to her, she suddenly seemed to go rigid. Softly, she said, "No, I suspect our friend with the herringbone sandals was carrying another dead body."

Gonda's head jerked up. Panic tensed his round face. "Herringbone sandals? You found something. Where?"

"What are you talking about?" Sindak asked. "He carries dead bodies?"

With her eyes still on the quill pattern, Koracoo instructed, "Show him, Sindak."

"Yes, War Chief." They stepped two paces away and knelt.

Towa stopped beside Koracoo. His long braid had come loose from its rabbit-bone skewer and hung over his cape like a black glistening rope. He squinted at Sindak and Gonda. "What are they looking for?"

"Another piece in a great mystery," she said. "Towa? The sandal tracks you found yesterday— did you see any evidence that the man was carrying something?"

Towa's handsome face went blank for several moments while he thought about it. "It's possible. There were several tracks where he'd slipped in the mud and had to regain his balance. He might have been struggling to balance something heavy."

Sindak and Gonda stood and returned.

Gonda said, "I swear those are the same sandal tracks we saw at the midden and the cornhusk doll meadow."

Koracoo nodded. For days now, she'd had the uneasy feeling that it was they who were being hunted. She'd dreamed last night that she was a snowshoe hare, running with a bursting heart, trying to reach a burrow before the wolves caught her. Were the Spirits trying to tell her something?

"Towa, you're a thinker. Think this through for

me. If these tracks, and the tracks you found yesterday, as well as the tracks Gonda and I found at the shell midden and the meadow, were all made by the same Hills People man, a man who carries dead bodies...what is he up to?"

Towa shrugged, but his eyes began darting over the sky and trees as he tried to figure it out. When he seemed to be having trouble, Sindak said, "Give Towa time; he'll figure it out. He really is a genius when it comes to analyzing information."

Towa gave Sindak *a for the sake of the Spirits, don't tell them that* look, and Sindak added. "Watch this. Towa, which of these things doesn't fit? A wolf, a fox, a dog, and a pile of shit in the middle of the plaza?"

Towa immediately answered, "The dog."

"The dog?" Gonda growled. "That's idiotic. Why?"

"Because dogs are the product of generations of careful breeding. Wolves, foxes, and the person who shit in the plaza, obviously are not."

Gonda and Koracoo stared at them.

"See?" Sindak said. "What did I tell you?"

Finally, Gonda said, "You know, these warrior things seem awfully complicated for you two. Maybe you should just trot along home and let us unravel the intrigue necessary for finding the children."

"You didn't think Towa was brilliant?" Sindak asked in genuine disbelief.

Gonda propped his hands on his hips. "Promise me something, will you? If you see some-body behind me with a bow, do *not* try to analyze the situation. Just yell. I'd rather learn about it through an incoherent cry than by choking on my own blood." He stalked away, back to kneel beside the sandal prints.

While Sindak and Towa muttered to each other, Koracoo concentrated on the sounds of the day. A riot of birdsong filled the trees, and the wind sawed lazily through the ice-crusted branches. Far in the distance, through a weave of trunks, Koracoo saw movement. She kept watching. The way they swayed, the bob of their heads, told her they were men.

"Find cover!" she ordered. "Now! Run for the trees!"

Gonda leaped up instantly and dashed away, his long legs stretching out, heading for the forest shadows. He was accustomed to such abrupt orders, but Sindak and Towa stared at her as though too stunned to move.

Koracoo growled, "I ordered you to run! *Run!*"

Both men seemed confused, but they charged after Gonda, disappearing into the trees.

Koracoo raced in the opposite direction, pounding along, and stamping out, the tracks they'd made this morning when they'd left the ramada. She ran up and back, confusing as much of the sign as she could in the time she had. It wouldn't help much, but it might force the enemy to stop long enough that she could kill them.

When she spied a pile of deadfall in a copse of sourgum trees, she dove behind it. The scent of damp, rotting wood filled her nostrils. A few scarlet leaves still clung to the branches and rattled in the breeze. From here, she could watch the trails in both directions and see across the clearing to where Gonda was hiding. And he would be watching her.

11

I t didn't take long.

Less than one thousand heartbeats later, two men trotted up the trail, coming from the east. They had their heads down, tracking. They would pass right by the ramada where Koracoo's party had made camp last night. The enemy warriors knew their prey was close.

Koracoo studied their plain buckskin capes and rabbit-fur leggings. They bore no clan symbols and had no distinctive designs that she could clearly identify as coming from any of the five Peoples south of Skanodario Lake. An old knife scar cut a white ridge across the tall man's ugly face. He was big, with muscular shoulders, and would be a formidable opponent if she had to face him. The other man, shorter and skinny to the point of looking starved, would be easier.

When they trotted to the place where she'd tried to obscure the trail, they stopped. They were less than twenty paces away.

The big man said, "The tracks go in both directions here."

"Yes, someone started running back and forth, as though panicked."

Skinny's gaze moved around the clearing, searching for hidden threats. He had a strangely narrow face, as though the bones had been pressed between boards when he'd been a baby. "Do you think these were made by people from Hawk Moth Village? Or is the old witch right and we're being followed?"

Hot blood surged through Koracoo's veins. The old witch? She clutched CorpseEye in a hard fist.

"I don't like this, Galan. If it weren't so lucrative, I'd say we just sell all the children and run home to our families."

Galan nodded. "Well, go, if you want to. But I'm staying. This war is making me rich. In another moon, I'll have enough goods to provide for my wife and children for the rest of my life." His gaze scanned the pile of deadfall where Koracoo hid. He seemed to sense something amiss in the shapes and colors. "Not only that, here I can do whatever I want to, and my clan can never find out. How often does a man have such freedom?"

"Don't you worry that someday you'll meet one

of the girls, and she'll be able to identify you? I do."
Hanu tapped the scar on his face. "Even twenty
summers from now, I'll still have this."

Galan laughed. "Gannajero never sells children without a guarantee that they'll be bashed in
the head when the buyers are finished with them.
By the time she lets them go, they've seen too much
to be allowed to live. Just make sure you do what
you want with them before she sells them."

The desire to kill consumed Koracoo's flesh at
the same time that grief drowned her heart.

These men were scouts. They must have been
dispatched to search out Gannajero's back trail.
That meant the children were not far ahead of
them. Her odds of rescuing them would substan-
tially improve if Gannajero had two fewer
warriors.

*All I have to do is follow their tracks right back
to her lair...*

Probably. But they'd lost the trails many times
before. Which meant she couldn't just kill them. A
pity.

She was shaking with rage when she laid
CorpseEye aside and nocked an arrow. Shifting
slightly, she aimed at the big man's chest, and let
fly. Before it had even struck his heart, she'd
grabbed Corpse-Eye, leaped the log, and was
pounding toward Galan.

The man saw her, cried, "No!" and raised his

war club. His feet kicked frost into the air as he charged her, screaming.

Koracoo lifted CorpseEye just as the man swung at her head. When their clubs met, it sounded like lightning cracking. He shoved her away, and Koracoo ducked, spun, and bashed him in the kidney.

"You bitch in heat!" he cried, and swung his war club blindly. "I'm going to kill you!"

Koracoo ducked the blow intended to crush her skull, and danced back. As she lifted CorpseEye again, the man shrieked a war cry and charged. She spun in low, cracking him across the kneecap. He staggered. Koracoo twirled and broke his right arm. Galan's war club dropped to the ground, but he didn't give up.

He shouted, "Gannajero will avenge my death!" and lunged for her, one hand shooting for her throat.

She didn't dodge fast enough. He body-slammed her to the ground and got his hand around her windpipe. As he squeezed, he said, "Does she have your children, bitch?"

Gasping for breath, Koracoo dropped Corpse-Eye, pulled a stiletto from her belt, and stabbed him repeatedly in the side and back. All the while, he howled and kept the pressure on her throat, strangling her.

Sindak and Towa raced toward her. Sindak

cried, "Make sure the big man is dead! I'll take care of the other one."

Sindak clubbed Galan in the head and pulled him off Koracoo.

Koracoo sat up, rubbing her injured throat.

Blood poured from Galan's head wound, but he managed to smile at Sindak. Sindak lifted his war club to kill him.

"No!" Koracoo shouted hoarsely. "Don't kill him, Sindak!"

Sindak whirled to stare at her in confusion, and she said, "They were...Gannajero's scouts...Make him...tell you...the meeting place."

Sindak's eyes flared. "Where are you supposed to meet Gannajero tonight, you piece of filth?"

Gonda ran by her, heading straight for the dying warrior, and fell to the ground at his side. He shouted in Galan's face, "Tell us! You have nothing to lose now! Tell me, and I'll make sure your family knows where your body is!"

Blood poured down Galan's face. He stared up at Gonda as though he couldn't quite see him. "Too late," he said. "You're...too late."

"Too late for what?"

Galan chuckled. "Children...all dead."

Gonda seemed to go weak. He straightened for a few instants; then he balled his fist and slammed it into Galan's face, shouting, "Liar! You're lying! Tell me you're lying!" Gonda kept hitting him.

Sindak didn't seem to know what to do. He stepped away, then glanced uneasily at Towa and Koracoo.

Koracoo got to her feet and, holding her throat, staggered toward Gonda. The dead warrior's face was bloody pulp, and Gonda was still slamming his fists into his face. She put a hand on Gonda's shoulder. "Stop. Gonda...stop! If we hurry, we should b-be..." She coughed violently. "Be able to track them right back to her camp."

Gonda swung around to look at her; then his gaze shifted to the clear tracks they'd left in the frost. "Blessed Spirits. Sindak? Towa? Take their weapons and their packs. We're leaving immediately!"

Sindak and Towa obeyed, ripping the men's packs from their shoulders and emptying their quivers.

Koracoo mustered her strength and walked over to pick up Corpse-Eye. After she tied the club to her belt, she wiped her sweating face on her cape. Her throat ached.

"Sindak," she ordered, "take the lead. If the trail forks, Gonda and I will follow one path; you and Towa will follow the other."

"Yes, Koracoo."

Sindak took off at a slow lope with Towa behind him.

She started to follow, but Gonda said, "Koracoo?" She turned.

"Forgive me." He unthinkingly threw his arms around her in a hard embrace, as he'd done a hundred times. "I'm sorry," he said. "I was almost too late."

Somewhere deep inside her, she heard Odion cry out, *"Mother!"* and she went rigid in Gonda's arms. He seemed to understand. Slowly, reluctantly, he released her and moved back.

They stared at each other. In Gonda's eyes, she saw barely endurable pain, and enough guilt to smother a nation. From the excruciating expression on his face, he must see in her eyes exactly what she was feeling: *nothing.* There was only emptiness in her heart. It wasn't natural. It was monstrous, and he did not understand it.

"Koracoo?" he said barely above a whisper. "Are you all right?"

"The frost is melting quickly, Gonda." She held a hand out to the trail. "Please, hurry."

12

ODION

Ash from the burning longhouses floats through the air like black snowflakes.

I shove food into my mouth as fast as I can. We sit on the shore of a river lined by white cedars and scrubby bladdernut trees. I've heard the warriors call it Quill River. The water is covered with ash and reflects the lurid light of dozens of campfires. There must be three or four hundred men here. For the first time ever, Gannajero gave us each a wooden bowl heaped with food: roasted dog meat, freshwater clams and mussels, boiled com gruel, squash, and dried plums. She must have Traded for it. Every warrior here swaggers around with a stuffed pack, smiling. More than a dozen games are in progress. Shouts and jeers fill the night. And there are many new children. Too many to count. Gannajero walks through them, selecting the ones she will keep. I try not to look. To feel.

The old woman ordered us not to say her name, and told us she'd slit our throats if we did. For tonight, she is "Lupan." A man. I study her blood-stained war shirt and ratty buckskin cape. Her toothless mouth is sunken in over her gums, but she frequently utters throaty laughs—just like the warriors. Her disguise includes a headdress made of long black hair and decorated with bright feathers. If I didn't know better, I'd be certain she was a man.

Wrass sits beside me, picking at his food. He places a single mussel in his mouth and chews slowly, as though it hurts to move his swollen jaw. His face looks even worse tonight than it did at dawn. The bruises have turned black. In the flickering firelight, his face almost seems to be covered with short-tailed weasel fur.

I say, "Bog Willow Village must have had plenty of food stored for winter."

He answers, "They won't need it any longer. Eat as much as you can hold."

I shove an entire handful of roasted dog into my mouth and chew. The meat is rich and tangy. My shrunken belly knots around it.

Tutelo leans her head against my shoulder and sighs as she sucks roast squash from her fingers.

Baji and Zateri have been sitting with their heads

together, eating while they whisper. Zateri has removed her bag of Spirit plants and tucked it beneath her leg. She keeps scanning the many cooking pots around the campfires. When she sees me looking at her, she silently picks up the bag and crawls over. "Hehaka is out serving the warriors. Maybe if I can get this bag to him, he can—"

"No," Wrass whispers. "We can't trust him. He's been here too long. He may think some of them are his friends."

I nod. "Wrass is right. One of us has to do it."

"Which one? How do we g-get close?" Zateri stutters, and her two front teeth seem to stick out farther.

I look around our small circle. All of us are terrified. No one wants to volunteer. Least of all me.

Wrass puts a hand to his head and closes his eyes as he weakly says, "Whoever does it will probably be killed. All of you need to understand. Tomorrow morning, they will start asking who was close to the pot. They'll figure it out, and they'll come looking for the person responsible."

"But Wrass," I say, "there are so many warriors here. There must be a thousand blood feuds between them. Why would they suspect us? I don't—"

"They will, Odion." Wrass slits his eyes and looks at me. "They will. Just accept it." He takes a breath and lets it out slowly. "The poison will only be in Gannajero's pot. They...they'll come after us first."

I doubt this, thinking she must have too many enemies to count, but I do not say it—because suddenly, clearly, I understand why Wrass insists the person who does it will die. That is the price. Whoever volunteers must be willing to sacrifice his or her life for the rest of us.

I shrink into myself. My shoulders hunch forward, and I stare at the ground. *Not me, gods. Please, not me.*

From my left, Tutelo rises. I jerk around to stare at her. She is standing tall, with her chin up and her tiny fists clenched at her sides. Half the copper ornaments are now gone from the sleeves and hem of her tan dress. Frayed threads hang loose. "I'll do it," she says. "I'm little. No one will be afraid of me."

I start to object, but Wrass cuts me off. "Tutelo, you are very brave. But I don't think—"

"Wrass, I'm just young, I'm not stupid. I can do it. But…but will you promise me something?"

"What, Tutelo?"

A strange glow lights her dark eyes. "I don't care what happens to me, but I want Odion to be safe. And Baji and Zateri. When the bad men start getting sick, can you get them away?"

"You would give yourself up? For them?" He has one eye closed, and slits the other.

Tears glisten on her lashes. "Yes, if you promise me you'll get them away. And get yourself away, too."

Wrass sucks in a deep breath and lets it out

slowly. As of tonight, he is our undisputed leader. Whatever he says, we will do. But he is very sick. He can barely hold his head up. "Why would you do that, Tutelo? You have only seen eight summers. Why would you give up the rest of your life for us?"

She squares her thin shoulders. "My mother is a war chief. She would give up her life for any of her warriors. I always wanted to be like her, to be a war chief someday." She looks around the circle. "I can do it, Wrass. I want to do it."

My heart aches. But I do not say a word. Fear is gnawing its way through my belly.

Zateri tucks the bag of Spirit plants into her leggings, edges forward, and puts a hand on my sister's arm. "Tutelo is brave, Wrass, but…I'm the one. I know how many Spirit plants to add, and I may be able to poison more than one pot. If I can do that, they won't automatically suspect us." She gazes out at the laughing warriors, and a mixture of fear and hatred tense her face. "The more of these men we can kill, the better. Maybe some of the new children can escape. And maybe all of you can escape."

Wrass asks, "Do you know what they'll do to you if they catch you?"

She lowers her eyes, and her face flushes. "I'm not going to lie to you. I'm scared to death of what they'll do…mostly scared of what they'll do before they kill me. But I can stand it, Wrass. If I know you're all safe, I can stand anything."

A faint smile touches Wrass' lips. "What if one of us gets injured escaping? He will need you and your Healing knowledge. I think you're the only one of us who is not expendable, Zateri."

Zateri's mouth quivers. "But I—"

"You're too valuable. Not you, Zateri."

He does not look my way, but I feel Wrass thinking about me. Waiting for me to volunteer.

Baji sits up straighter, girding herself, and smooths her long black hair away from her face. She knows from firsthand experience what the warriors will do to her before they kill her.

Baji says, "Me. I'm the one, Wrass. I'll do it."

"You?" I say. "Why—"

Wrass grasps my arm to stop me from continuing. He nods at Baji. "Baji may be the only one of us who can get close enough."

"Why do you think that?" I demand to know.

With tears in her eyes, Baji answers, "Because, silly boy, I'm beautiful. I can make the men want me enough that they'll carry me right into their camp and sit me down by the stew pot. No matter what happens, by the end of the night, I *will* have dumped the Spirit plants in Gannajero's pot." Her eyes are stony, resolved to do what must be done to save the rest of us.

Wrass studies her for a long time before he asks, "Are you sure about this, Baji?"

"Yes, it's...it's for my sisters. If I die, you'll carry

my bones home, won't you? So I can travel to the afterlife to be with them?"

Wrass' eyes glitter. "If I have breath in my body, I will find and carry your bones back to your people. I give you my oath."

A trembling smile comes to Baji's lips. She holds out her hand. "Give me the Spirit plants, Zateri."

Zateri pulls the bag from her leggings and hesitantly hands it over. "Baji, if you can, only use half the bag in Gannajero's pot, then—"

"No." Baji shakes her head. "I want her dead. I'm going to dump it all in. I can't wait to see her writhing on the ground, clutching at her throat and vomiting her guts out."

Zateri swallows hard. "All right."

Wrass' head doesn't move, but his gaze shifts. He looks at me with haunted eyes.

Pain constricts my heart like strips of wet rawhide drying in the heat of Elder Brother Sun. He's already chosen Baji, hasn't he? What could it hurt to tell him I'll go? He wouldn't pick me. He's already said that she's the only one who can get close enough. He wouldn't pick me...would he?

I sit as though made of ice.

Wrass lowers his gaze and looks away. The firelight casts the long shadow of his hooked nose across his cheek. "All right, Baji. You're the one. But you can't do it until later. After the warriors have been drinking corn brew and fighting for half the night, their guards will be down. I'll tell you when. Agreed?"

Baji nods. "Yes."

Wrass hangs his injured head. "Let's all finish eating and get as much rest as we—"

Kotin appears out of the crowd and walks toward us with two men. All are swaying on their feet, laughing and shoving each other. Having a good time.

When he stops before us, Kotin bares his broken yellow teeth and says, "You, Chipmunk Teeth, go with Pestis. He'll take good care of you."

Zateri starts shaking.

Pestis staggers forward. He is short and squat. His eyes are rolling in his head, as though he can't keep them still. "Come here, girl!"

Zateri seems to have petrified. She just stares at him with her jaw clenched.

Kotin lunges for her, grabs her arm, and hauls her to her feet. "I said go with Pestis!" He shoves her into Pestis' arms.

Her legs are trembling when Pestis drags her out into the forest, far away from the camp.

Not even victorious warriors would couple with a child. Gannajero must have sent out advance scouts to move through the war party and find the men with dangerous appetites. Or, perhaps these men do not know Zateri and Baji are still girls? Has Gannajero told them they are women? Baji could be mistaken for a woman, but Zateri...

"You, Standing Stone boy," Kotin says, and I jerk around to stare at him. "Go with War Chief Manidos."

The muscular giant squints at me and says, "He's a skeleton. Don't you ever feed them? I don't want him. What about the other boy? At least he has some muscles on his body."

Kotin eyes Wrass. Wrass glares defiantly at him and braces his hands on the ground to stand.

Kotin says, "We beat him half to death last night. He'll just throw up all over you."

"Oh, well…" The giant's lips pucker. "All right, I'll take the skeleton."

I do not move.

"Get up, boy," Kotin orders.

"No!" Tutelo cries and runs forward. She throws herself at Kotin, slamming her fists into his legs. "Leave my brother alone! Leave him alone!"

"You little wildcat." Kotin puts a hand on her head and shoves her hard to the ground.

Tutelo starts wailing in a high-pitched voice I've never heard before.

"Tutelo!" I cry and leap to my feet to run to her.

But Kotin catches me by the back of the shirt and swings me around and right into the giant's arms. Kotin smiles. "We've been saving him for you, Manidos. He's fresh. You'll like him. If you don't, I'll refund half the price."

Manidos crushes my hand in his and drags me

away into the forest. My heart is thundering. He's in a hurry, walking fast, trying to get far away from the camp. I can't keep up and keep tripping over rocks and roots. Each time, he hauls me to my feet without a word.

13

Gonda trotted in the lead. Ahead, black smoke billowed into the night sky, creating what appeared to be a massive thunderhead that blotted out the campfires of the dead.

The People of the Dawnland called their country Ndakinna, meaning "our land," and it was a beautiful place, filled with towering tree-covered mountains and rushing rivers. Despite the stench of smoke, red cedars, firs, and black spruces scented the air with sweetness.

He slowed down to trot beside Koracoo. Her short black hair clung to her cheeks, matted by sweat. They'd been running most of the day. "The war party may still be there."

She nodded. "They will certainly be close by.

Be especially careful. We are all so tired we're shaky and vulnerable."

Gonda forced his wobbly legs to climb the steep trail and trotted through thick pines. When he reached the crest of the hill, he saw the burning village. The sight was stunning. There had to be over one hundred houses. The pole frames had collapsed into heaps, and flames leaped fifty hands into the air above them. Koracoo stopped beside him. In the firelight, her flushed face looked like pure gold. She didn't say a word. She just looked out over the horrifying vista.

"Blessed gods," Gonda said. "I had no idea Bog Willow Village was so big."

Koracoo took a deep breath and coughed, then rubbed her throat. "A Trader once told me over one thousand people lived here."

By Standing Stone standards, the Dawnland People had a crude, backward culture. Their houses were partially subterranean pit dwellings made by digging a hole in the ground twenty-five hands long and around twenty wide, then erecting a pole frame over the top and covering the oval structure with bark. They lived in their pit dwellings from fall through spring, but abandoned them in the summer to fish the many lakes and streams and gather plant resources.

"The attack was brutal," he said softly, and scanned the hundreds of bodies that littered the ground. Crushed baskets, broken pots, and other belongings were strewn everywhere, probably kicked by racing feet.

"To make matters more complicated," Koracoo said, "there will be survivors roaming the forest, waiting for a chance to kill any enemy warrior they find."

"Which means us."

Sindak and Towa stopped beside them, breathing hard, and stared out at the devastation. Sindak's sharp gaze moved across the village, then out to the blackened spruces that fringed the plaza, and finally westward to the endless blue mountains. "Who attacked them?"

Koracoo answered, "Flint People, probably. They've never gotten along with the Dawnland People. Let's continue on."

She broke into a trot again, taking the lead.

As they moved closer, the gaudy orange halo swelled to fill the entire sky, and ash fell like black snowflakes, coating their hair and capes.

Gonda said, "This happened just a few hands of time ago."

They veered wide around the burning houses, passing them from less than fifty paces, close enough to see that most of the bodies lay sprawled facedown, as though they'd been shot in the backs as they'd fled. The stench of torn intestines was redolent on the wind.

Gonda trotted by the last burning house and out onto the main trail that led south. He'd gone no more than two hundred paces when he saw a new orange gleam in the distance.

He slowed down and lifted his arm to point. "If that is a warriors' camp, it's huge."

Sindak frowned. "Are you sure it's not another village?"

Koracoo said, "It's a warriors' camp."

Towa shook sweat-soaked hair out of dark eyes and said, "We lost the children's trail two hands of time ago when it was obliterated by thousands of footprints, but it was heading right for this village. Do you think Gannajero was bringing the children here to meet the victorious warriors?"

Gonda's knees trembled. *Don't think about it.* He stiffened his muscles to still them and replied, "Victorious warriors always have plunder in their packs. That's why Traders follow war parties. If I—"

Koracoo interrupted him. "Let's stop talking and find out."

She loped toward the orange gleam. Gonda, Sindak, and Towa fell into line behind her.

14

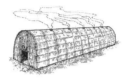

In the middle of the night, Wrass lifted his head and looked around. There was only one guard, Tenshu. The warrior had his back to Wrass, watching Gannajero and Kotin. The old woman stood thirty paces from her fire. In her ratty buckskin cape and long black wig, she looked so much like a toothless old man that it astonished him. She was haggling with an ugly little Flint warrior and gesturing to the new children. She'd selected five. They sat in a group, roped together, crying. Gannajero kept shouting and shaking her head. Kotin, who stood at her side, held his war club in a tight grip. No one was sitting around her fire. The pot stood unwatched.

Wrass studied Tenshu from the corner of his eye. Gannajero must have figured that Hehaka, two girls, and an injured boy wouldn't be a problem for one trained warrior. He glanced at Hehaka, Tutelo, and Baji. Despite the noise and shouts, they slept soundly eight hands away. His gaze moved over Hehaka, to the girls. They were pretty. Especially Baji. She was lying on her back. A dark halo of long black hair spread around her face. In another time and place, Wrass might have asked his grandmother if he could court her.

Grandmother's dead.

Tenshu chuckled softly, apparently amused by Gannajero's contorted face and waving sticklike arms.

Wrass slid over and pulled the bag from Baji's leggings. She was so tired, she didn't even move. He tucked it into his moccasin and rolled onto his hands and knees. The pain in his head almost flattened him. He closed his eyes for several moments and concentrated on breathing in the cold night air. It took all his strength to stifle the urge to vomit. When he felt a little better, he reached for a rock twice the size of his fist and clutched it in his hand as he rose to his feet.

As quiet as morning mist, he sneaked up behind Tenshu, who was laughing out loud now... and slammed the rock into the back of his skull. The warrior let out a surprised grunt. When he whirled, Wrass hit him in the temple as hard as he could. Tenshu staggered, trying to swing his war club at Wrass, but his arms had no strength. Wrass slammed the rock right into Tenshu's forehead.

Tenshu staggered backward, then dropped to his knees. Wrass hit him over and over, until he heard the man's skull crack. Wrass stopped only when Tenshu collapsed facefirst to the ground, and his limbs started violently twitching and jerking.

Baji, Hehaka, and Tutelo scrambled up and were staring at Wrass with wide eyes. Tutelo started to cry, or scream, but Baji clamped a hard hand over her mouth and hissed, "Quiet, Tutelo! Be quiet."

Hehaka was watching with wide, luminous eyes, as though he couldn't believe that anyone could kill one of Gannajero's men.

Wrass tossed the rock aside and wiped his bloody hand on his cape. When he'd managed to stiffen his legs and stand up straight, he said to Baji, "Run."

"What?" she said in confusion.

"Run. Now. All of you. Don't stop. By dawn there will be so many tracks leading out of here that they'll never be able to track you."

"But I—" Baji reached for the bag in her leggings. "Where's my bag? I'm the one—"

"I'll do it. Now, for the sake of the gods, go."

Baji grabbed Tutelo's hand and lunged to her feet.

Hehaka rose unsteadily beside them. "But... where will we go? Who will feed us?"

Wrass' eyes narrowed. Was the boy totally unable to care for himself? "Baji will help you."

Tutelo struggled against Baji's grip, crying, "But where's Odion? I can't leave without Odion! Where's my brother?"

"I'll wait for Odion. You have to go, Tutelo," Wrass said. "Hurry. I'll take care of Gannajero and her men, kill them all, right down to the last breath in my body. But you have to save yourselves, or it will mean nothing. Do you understand? My life for yours. That's the Trade. Now, please, get out of here before I lose my nerve."

Baji looked at Wrass with so much admiration in her dark eyes it made him a little dizzy. She tightened her hold on Tutelo's hand and vowed, "I'm coming back for you, Wrass. And I'm bringing a war party with me. Come on, Tutelo. Hehaka? Move!"

Tutelo opened her mouth to cry, but no sounds came out. Finally, she whimpered, "Tell Odion I love him. Tell him!"

Wrass nodded. "I'll tell him."

Baji dragged Tutelo out into the trees and trotted away. Hehaka ran after her, but he kept looking back at the camp, probably searching for Gannajero. The darkness swallowed them.

Wrass staggered. The pain was almost too

much to bear. He longed to lie down and weep. Worse, he was having trouble seeing. The campfires were blurs amid a sea of moving bodies and drifting smoke.

He forced his shaking legs to carry him over to Tenshu. After he dragged the warrior's club from his dead hand, he had to lean against a tree trunk to keep standing.

"I can do this," he hissed to himself. "I just need...to breathe...for a moment."

He thought about his father, whom he'd watched die at Yellowtail Village. The arrow had struck Father in the leg, slicing through the big artery. It hadn't taken long for him to bleed to death...but it had seemed like it.

Wrass hefted the war club, testing its weight. It was almost too heavy for him to wield effectively. Sucking in one last fortifying breath, he looked up at the campfires of the dead and whispered, "Please, meet me at the bridge, Father."

Then he slipped back into the trees and staggered through the shadows, heading for Gannajero's campfire.

15

Sindak looked across at Towa, then past him to Gonda and Koracoo. All four of them had flattened out on their bellies on the rocky hilltop overlooking the enormous warriors' camp that stretched along the western bank of the Quill River. Over one hundred fires burned, and each was encircled by a rowdy group of triumphant warriors talking, eating, and laughing too loudly. A group of captive children, roped together, huddled to the west, near the tree line, and on the northern outskirts of the camp, four fistfights raged.

Sindak slid sideways across the frozen grass toward Towa and remarked, "This is worse than the Wolf Clan longhouse at midnight."

Towa kept his gaze on the camp. "You're just jealous because my clan is the largest and the oldest."

"Yes, well, the person who said that being really old was a virtue had seen sixteen summers. Large, however—that could have been any male."

Towa ignored him. "From this distance, I can't see very clearly. How many warriors are down there?"

"I'd guess around four hundred, maybe five."

"Are they all Flint People?"

"Most are. But I see Mountain and Landing warriors, too."

Towa turned to stare Sindak in the eyes. "So, if we walk in there and try to grab a few children, we'll be dead in less than ten heartbeats."

"I'd say five."

Towa's mouth quirked. "Do you have any helpful ideas?"

"No. How about you?"

Towa rubbed the back of his neck as though the muscles had knotted up. "Well, if I run hard for ten or twelve days, I should be home."

Sindak nodded. "When you get there, put in a good word for me, will you? My clan matron, Tila, thinks I'm a coward."

"Sindak, I doubt that even your glorious death will be enough to convince—"

"*Towa,*" Gonda whispered, as though to shut them up.

They both turned to watch him sliding toward them on his belly. Ash had settled on Gonda's heavy brow, filling in the lines of his forehead like black paint. His chopped-off black hair stuck to his wide cheekbones. "We're moving closer. Nock your bows."

"Closer?" Sindak said. "Why? So they can see the whites of our eyes when they kill us?"

Gonda scowled at him. "We're not going to get that close, imbecile. There's enough firelight that if we spot the children, we may be able to shoot their guards and sneak in and rescue them before anyone knows it."

Towa glanced uneasily at the camp. "Forgive me, but even if our children are there, they're surrounded by hundreds of warriors. We'll never—"

"Look at me, Towa." Gonda glowered. "Try to forget your own hide. We're going to circle around the western edge of the camp, then work our way north through the trees, staying about ten paces apart. Do you understand?"

Towa's brows knitted over his straight nose. "Of course."

Koracoo ordered, "Nock your bows. We're leaving."

She slid backward down the hill and trotted for the cover of the spruces. Gonda gave them one last hostile glance before he rose to follow her.

Sindak pulled an arrow from his quiver and pointed it suggestively at Towa's chest. "Concentrate, and you may actually get lucky and hit what you're aiming at."

Towa smiled and turned to the camp again. Warriors' faces gleamed with a rose-amber hue, and the echoes of laughter and songs rang through the night—but the whimpers of children and screams of the wounded thrummed beneath the revelry.

As Towa nocked his bow, he said, "It's a good day to die. But I don't plan on it."

16

ODION

I sit with my teeth chattering. Manidos lies flat on his back, snoring, two paces away. I can't seem to keep my head still. It keeps jerking, as though my backbone is injured. I saw a deer do this once. Father's bow shot had gone high, slicing the buck just below the spine. When the animal fell, its antlered head continued to jerk and thrash until it died. Father said his arrow must have damaged the deer's backbone. I reach around to touch my lower back. I can't tell. Everything hurts.

I glance around like a stunned owl. I should run… I…should. But I only have the strength to pull Manidos' blanket close below my jerking chin. Manidos gave me the blanket. He said it was a present because I'd been a good boy.

A few hundred warriors stagger about and laugh. The sounds of drums and flutes fill the air. Perhaps another one hundred warriors sit before fires, eating bowls of food. I smell the rich scents of roasted duck and sacred tobacco smoke on the night wind. Every color in the rainbow shines in the firelight. I see pure white doehide capes, and pure black capes decorated with seashells. Porcupine quillwork glimmers, and polished copper ornaments blaze. And their jewelry! Every throat is encircled with strings of beads, etched copper and human skull gorgets, and a wealth of bear claw and elk ivory necklaces.

I see Wrass. He is standing with his cold hands extended to Gannajero's fire, warming them. His face is swollen and bruised. One of his eyes is half-closed. A war club is tucked into his belt…Why is he free? Did Gannajero release him?

A sudden cold wave flushes my body. *Where's Tutelo?*

I struggle to my feet just as Wrass starts walking back toward our place in the forest, and I stumble toward him, through the trees, paralleling his path. He doesn't see me for a long time. Then he whirls and stares into the trees as though he knows someone is there.

I call, "Wrass? It…it's me."

"Odion?"

I stagger into the open, and relief slackens Wrass' hideous face. He says, "Thank the gods," and runs to me.

He hugs me hard, and I start to cry against his

shoulder, terrible wrenching tears that make me feel as though I'm suffocating. "Wr-Wrass, I—I'm hurt."

"I know, Odion. But you're alive." He strokes my hair, and in a strong voice, says, "Listen to me. We have to run. This is our chance. Can you do it?"

He backs away and stares down into my eyes. It's as if the strength in his body is flowing into me through his gaze. I can feel it. My heart starts to beat harder. Hot blood surges through my veins.

I swallow hard and say, "Why haven't you already run? You should be gone!"

"I couldn't leave you here by yourself, Odion. Now, let's—"

Frantically, I grab his arm and say, "Where's Tutelo? Is she—"

"Right after I killed Tenshu, I told Baji to take her and run. She said to tell you she loves you. She should be far away by now, which is where you and I need to be."

I stare dumbly at him. "But where…"

Over Wrass' shoulder, I see Kotin suddenly look toward the clearing where we'd been sitting. Confusion lines his face. He says something to Gannajero, who waves him away and continues haggling for the new children while Kotin stalks toward the clearing.

"Wrass?" I hiss. "Kotin…he's…"

Wrass swings around to follow my gaze, sees Kotin, and orders, "Odion, move! Start walking; don't run."

"You lead. You—you lead, Wrass, please?"

Wrass moves past me and heads out into the dark trees, following a deer trail. I try to stay no more than one pace behind him, but his legs are longer than mine. I have to half-run to keep up. Wrass is breathing hard, and he's put one hand to his head, as though he's sick, but he moves swiftly along the trail, winding between enormous chestnuts and pines that seem to pierce the smoky belly of Brother Sky.

Behind us, I hear Kotin let out a sharp cry; then he shouts, "Tenshu's dead! The children have escaped! Waswan? Gather four of our new men and get over here!"

Neither of us turns around. Wrass walks until we're out of sight of the camp; then he starts running. We lunge down the trail, panting, scrambling through a thicket of nannyberry shrubs, running with all the strength in our bodies. Ahead of us, a scrubby grove of prickly ash trees stands out like a cluster of spikes. Old autumn leaves have blown around the bases of the trees and created a pile ten hands deep and forty hands across.

Within moments, feet pound behind us, the heavy steps like a staccato of arrows thumping a longhouse wall, coming up the deer trail.

Wrass casts a glance over his shoulder and stops dead in the trail.

"What are you doing?" I cry in terror. "Keep running!"

Wrass grabs my hand, places the war club in it, then hisses in my face, "Hide in those leaves, Odion. If they find you, swing the club as hard as you can, and don't stop swinging. No matter what you hear or see, keep swinging. Do you hear me? I'm going to lead them away. I'll meet you at the fire cherry camp at dawn."

"But Wrass, I'm scared. I want to go with you! Let me—"

He growls, "I told you to hide. Now do it!" Wrass shoves me hard in the direction of the prickly ashes, and he breaks into a run.

I careen forward, stumble into the spiky trunks, and bury myself in the deep leaves.

I hear shouts. Men calling to each other.

The pungent scent of the moldering leaves surrounds me. I try not to breathe, or move. I see nothing. Pitch darkness. The leaves rustle softly when I blink my eyes. I should close them...but I can't. I must keep watch, even if only on the blackness.

"The filthy brats!" Kotin snarls. His feet bang against the trail. As he approaches my hiding place, I feel his steps in my bones. I tighten my grip on the war club. Another man runs behind him. His steps are lighter, more like a dancer's. "I wager it was that older boy, the one with the hawk face. I knew he was going to be a problem."

"He killed one of your best warriors, Kotin. He's no longer a boy. He's become a man," Waswan said.

"In just a few moments, he's going to be a *dead* man."

"He's Gannajero's property. I'd think hard about that."

"Well, come on!" Kotin growls. "He's injured. He can't be that far ahead of us. Gannajero will flay our skin from our bodies if we don't catch them."

"She'll really miss the two girls."

Their steps pound away up the trail, heading in the same direction as Wrass.

Relief makes me weak. Breath escapes my lungs in a rush, and the leaves crackle and resettle over my face.

Please, gods, let Tutelo and Baji get away! Let Wrass escape!

Painful, horrifying images of Yellowtail Village, burning, flash behind my eyes: people running... screams...flaming arrows arcing through the sky as I clutch Tutelo's hand and duck through the hole in the palisade wall to emerge in a big group of children and elders...then the mad rush into the forest, tripping, falling, Tutelo shrieks...warriors all around...nowhere to—

Odion?

I go rigid.

The voice is inhuman, the haunting song of wolves on a blood trail.

Odion. Follow me.

Sobs choke me. My eyes squeeze closed in terror. How does he know my name?

Follow me, Odion.

As though my body is moving without my souls willing it, I brace one hand on the ground and I'm rising up, leaves cascading away from me. I sit amid the prickly ash saplings, holding the war club across my lap. After the blackness, the firelit forest seems almost bright.

"Where are you?" I call.

I'm here.

I see him. Shago-niyoh...the Child. Leaning against the trunk of a chestnut. A dark hooded figure. Is it a man? Or a Forest Spirit? He's tall, broad-shouldered. Inside his hood there is only midnight.

Follow me, Odion, he says again, and turns in a sable whirl of cape and heads away through the forest, his steps soundless.

I look around. There is no other choice. I could try to find Wrass, but the warriors will be right behind him now. He may already be dead.

I stand on shaking legs and clench the war club to will courage into my terrified souls. Then I rise and stumble after him through leaf-covered rocks, and over slippery piles of deadfall. Shago-niyoh stays twenty or thirty paces ahead of me, close enough that I can keep following, but never close enough that I can really see him.

When I lurch through a tangle of old vines, I

stumble and lose him. The snow-tipped black pine needles reflect the firelight, giving the forest a strange, unearthly shimmer.

"Shago-niyoh?" The forest seems to be closing in around me, the trees bending down to stare at me.

A footfall rustles; a sandal crunches in leaves. *Warriors!*

I spin around on the verge of screaming...but I see only a faintly darker splotch in the night forest. Does he have a hump on his back? Is he an old man? As he moves away, on down the trail, he seems to walk hunched over, and there may be a walking stick in his hand. Clicks accompany his steps, like a stick tapping the ground—or claws on rocks.

I rush after him.

In less than two hundred heartbeats, he's far ahead of me. Very far. I can barely see him. I run, trying to catch up.

Silent as a shadow, he slides through the nightmare of dark trees, and I swear he's flying now, sailing between the trunks like an owl on a hunt. Wings whisper...but is the sound coming from him, or somewhere else in the canopy?

Tears trace warm lines down my cheeks. I batter my way through brush, fighting to keep sight of him... and my heart goes cold and dead in my chest.

Ahead, on the deer trail, are four warriors. Coming my way. He's led me right to a group of warriors. They are marching two girls in front of them, and I recognize Tutelo's walk. Her head is down. Baji walks beside her, holding her hand. Then I see Hehaka to Baji's left.

I spin around to look for Shago-niyoh. Where is he? Why did he bring me here? Why doesn't he do something? Tutelo is his friend, isn't she?

My gaze flits through the forest, stopping on every shadow, searching for him. Trees sway in the cold wind. Brush rattles.

He has abandoned me.

As the warriors get closer, I hear Tutelo crying... and Hehaka laughing.

17

Veils of smoke blew around Koracoo's tall body, drifting past Sindak, who walked ten paces behind her. He cast a glance over his shoulder and saw Gonda and Towa appear and disappear amid the trees. The tempting smells of roasting meat and frying cornmeal balls pervaded the air.

Despite the raucous voices, the clattering of pots, and banging of horn spoons against wooden bowls, there was a strange silence in the wavering firelit shadows of the forest. Wind Mother had stilled to a barely discernible breath, quieting the branches. No owls or night herons called. Sindak's steps upon the pine needles were ghostly, almost not there.

They had cut across two main game trails as they'd wound around the western side of the camp, and now approached a third. Koracoo took a moment to look down; then she aimed her nocked bow at the trail, telling Sindak to look when he passed, and she continued on.

Sindak slowly made his way to the trail. No wonder she'd wanted him to see. Small footprints covered the mud. Even in the dim firelight, he could tell the children had been running. His gaze followed the deer trail as it curved out into the trees, and his pulse sped up. Reflected firelight danced like leaping giants in the tamarack boughs. He swiveled to look back at the camp, where around thirty children sat—five huddled in a knot, roped together. The braided hide ropes around their necks and hands shone—then his gaze shifted back to the deer trail. Had the running children escaped?

He heard Gonda's steps closing in behind him, no more than five paces away, and Koracoo had gotten twenty paces ahead. Sindak aimed his bow at the trail, telling Gonda to look, and continued on. He had to hurry if he was going to—

Koracoo stopped. It was as though she'd suddenly turned to stone. She was so still her black hair caught the light and held it like an obsidian mirror. Deer did that—froze suddenly at the sight or sound of a predator.

Sindak held his breath, waiting to see or hear what had alarmed Koracoo.

In less than five heartbeats, four warriors carelessly walked up the deer trail. They were still fifty paces away. He glimpsed them as they weaved between the dark trunks of the trees. The men were joking with each other, chuckling as they herded two girls and a boy before them. One kept reaching forward to fondle the older girl's small breasts, while the little boy laughed.

Sindak saw Koracoo subtly pull back her bowstring and aim in the men's direction. He did the same. Behind him, Towa and Gonda had gone silent.

Just as the warriors rounded a bend in the game trail, a bloodcurdling childish shriek tore the air.

Sindak jerked, trying to see where it had come from, but he—

Thirty paces ahead, a thin little boy ran out of the trees, onto the trail, and launched himself at the lead warrior, swinging a war club that was much too heavy for him. He was off balance, struggling, but he surprised the lead warrior and landed a solid blow across the man's left wrist. Sindak could hear it snap from where he stood. The warrior bawled, "He broke my wrist!"

The three other warriors lunged forward, but the boy didn't run. He swung the war club with wild fury and cried, "Tutelo! Baji! Run! Run!"

From behind Sindak, Gonda shouted, "Odion?

Odion!" and the name rang with a familiarity that shocked Sindak.

The warrior who chased me called that name.

The taller girl grabbed the other's hand and fled into the forest as the attacking boy ducked a blow aimed at his head, brought his war club around, and cracked it across his attacker's left hip. The enraged warrior let out a roar as he staggered sideways and bellowed, "You're dead, boy!" He lifted his club over his head and swung it down, but the boy parried the blow, though it knocked him flat on his back on the ground.

Gonda shoved past Sindak with his war club in his fist, rushing to get into the fight.

Koracoo shouted, "Gonda, no! Use your bow!"

Gonda ignored her. From the expression on his face, he wanted to kill these men with his own hands.

Sindak leveled his bow, but before he could let fly, Koracoo's and Towa's arrows flashed through the air in front of him. Towa's missed and splintered against a tree. Koracoo's lanced through the shoulder of the man with the broken wrist, thrust him backward into his friend, and threw the second man right into Sindak's line of fire. He loosed his arrow, and it struck the man in the left lung. As he staggered, clutching at the shaft in his chest, Gonda leaped and bashed in his rib cage; then he whirled and landed a deadly blow to the throat of the man with the broken wrist. He yelled, "Odion, get out of the way!"

The boy parried another blow that drove his war club into his chest and, as though in disbelief, cried, *"Father?"*

The boy's attacker lifted his club for the death blow, and Koracoo rushed forward, twisting, leaping, and swinging her legendary war club so fast that her movements became a supernatural dance. She spun and crushed the spine of Odion's opponent, then kicked his feet out from under him and brought CorpseEye down across the bridge of his nose with a shattering *whump.*

The last warrior pulled a stiletto from his belt and leaped upon Gonda, knocking his war club from his hand. Both men landed hard on the ground, rolling, kicking, trying to gain leverage over the other.

The boy, Odion, staggered to his feet and stared at Koracoo. He looked stunned, like a clubbed animal. Koracoo ran past him to help Gonda.

Gonda's opponent managed to get on top and was trying to gouge out Gonda's eyes when Sindak calmly nocked another arrow and shot Gonda's opponent through the head just as Koracoo swung CorpseEye to kill him. The man dropped on top of Gonda like a rock. CorpseEye sliced through thin air above him.

Panting, Gonda shoved the dead man away and clambered to his feet. He pivoted to look at Sindak, who still had his bow up, and gave him a grateful nod.

"Father?" The boy blinked at Gonda. "M-Mother?"

Gonda staggered to the boy, dropped to his knees, and embraced him hard enough to drive the air from his young lungs, saying, "Odion. Odion, I told you I'd find you."

From behind a tree trunk, the other little boy stepped out and stood gaping at them. He had a starved face, with dark eyes and a flat nose. "You killed them!" he said. "Who are you?"

In the camp, men had started to stand up. They must have heard the commotion and suspected it was more than an ordinary fistfight. A few warriors started drifting in their direction.

Koracoo ordered, "Towa, Sindak, help Gonda get the children to safety. I'm going after Tutelo and the other girl. I'll meet you at the overlook hill." She ran past Gonda and her son and lunged onto the trail with her feet flying.

Contrary to orders, Sindak was right behind her, pounding into the trees.

18

A sudden cold tingling sensation made Gannajero turn away from the man she was negotiating with and stare out at the clearing where Hehaka and the children who were not working should be sleeping. The wind had come up. Branches swayed and glimmered in the firelight. She did not see Tenshu standing guard.

"Ojib? Where's Tenshu?"

He turned toward the clearing. Ojib was of medium height, but wide across the shoulders, built like a bull moose. His nose had been broken one too many times and spread across his flat face like a squashed plum. "Kotin went to check on him. He's supposed to be guarding the—"

"Go find him."

"Yes, Lupan." Ojib broke into a trot just as

several men on the western edge of camp rose to their feet and started heading in that direction.

The short, ugly little Flint warrior she'd been negotiating with, Tagohsah, said, "Throw in another five shell gorgets and they are yours." The sides of his head had been shaved, leaving the characteristic single ridge of hair down the middle of his skull. He'd decorated the roach with white shell beads.

"Five?" Gannajero scoffed. She glared at the roped children, who looked up at her with tear-filled eyes. They were *beautiful*. Worth a fortune to the men who craved them. "I'll give you three," she said.

"Done." Tagohsah gleefully rubbed his hands together. His anxious gaze flicked to her pack where it rested by her feet.

Gannajero knelt to retrieve the payment. As she pulled out the gorgets and tossed them onto the pile, she saw Kotin. He was walking in from the southern edge of the camp with Waswan, shoving the beaten hawk-faced boy before him. The boy had his jaw clenched. His hands were tied behind him.

Tagohsah chuckled. "It's a pleasure selling to you, Lupan. You have a good eye for child slaves. These are top quality." He knelt and began scooping the pile of wealth into his own pack.

Gannajero rose to her feet, and locks of long black hair swung around her wrinkled face.

Ojib had reached the clearing, along with two other men, and shouts rang out. Ojib bent down, as though examining something on the ground, then rose to his feet, looked at her, and ran back. The other two men remained standing over whatever lay upon the ground.

When Ojib arrived, he said, "Tenshu is dead. The children are gone."

"That's impossible!" she exclaimed. Rage flooded her veins. She pointed to her pack. "Pick that up; then find Chipmunk Teeth, rope her with the others, and meet me at our camp."

"Yes, Lupan."

She tramped across the camp to meet Kotin and Waswan. The hawk-faced boy glared at her as she approached. Kotin flashed broken, yellow teeth and called, "We caught him! Are the others back yet?"

"What others?"

Kotin's grin faded. He'd been with her for moons and could probably tell his life was teetering in the balance. "The Mountain warriors you hired this afternoon. They went after the girls and Hehaka."

The rage in her body burned like fire. "Hehaka is gone, too? I told you he was the *one* child that would cost you your life if he ever escaped!"

Kotin threw up his hands and cried, "I'll find him, Ga—Lupan! I thought he'd already be back. Just give me—"

Her attention shifted to the northern hill that sloped down to the river. Tilted slabs of rock jutted up between the spruces, ashes, and white walnut trees. She hated Dawnland country; it was little more than densely clustered mountain ranges cut by an endless number of rivers, streams, and creeks. It was exhausting to traverse.

She squinted. Something moved there—a glimmer. She scanned the hill carefully. In the sky beyond the hilltop, the campfires of the dead blazed and vanished through the drifting smoke.

Gannajero started to look back at Kotin—but she *had* seen a glimmer. A cold shiver passed through her when it appeared again.

The blue sparkle moved among the spruces, disappeared, then flashed again farther east, as though walking down toward the dozens of canoes bunched at the river landing.

"Kotin? Do you see that?" She pointed.

"See what?"

"On the hilltop, you fool. Look!"

The sparkle flashed again in the branches of a mountain ash tree. "There! See?"

Kotin shrugged and shook his head. "I don't see anything."

Breathing hard, she clenched her jaw. She

couldn't take her gaze from the scrubby ashes. Then, for a brief instant, the glimmer became two fiery eyes, and the hair on her arms stood on end. She could *feel* him staring directly at her. He seemed to materialize out of nothingness—a shape, blacker than the background sky, tall, wearing a long cape. His hood buffeted in the wind.

Then he was gone.

Gannajero lifted a hand to clutch her constricted throat. "We're heading south immediately, Kotin. Gather the slaves. Collect our payments."

"South?" Kotin said. "Into the lands of the People Who Separated? But we've never—"

"That's why we're going there! No one knows us. Find a Trader. Buy us two canoes, and let's be on our way."

Kotin shrank back from her anger. "Shall I hunt for the missing girls and Hehaka first, or—"

"I said we're heading south *now*. Forget them!"

"All right. I understand. I'll get things organized. But none of us have eaten, Lupan. We've been so busy trading—"

"That's true." Waswan nodded. He was sapling thin and looked half-starved. He held Hawk-Face's sleeve. "I'm hungry."

"The stew pot at our campfire is full. Feed the men quickly!"

Kotin backed away from her with his hands up.

"Right away, Lupan. Come on, Waswan. You can help me collect our last payments; then we'll eat and leave."

They trotted into the center of the camp, calling orders, and assembling the new men she'd hired. Most trotted for the pot to eat, while Kotin and Waswan worked through the camp, collecting payments, dragging Hawk-Face with them. The boy was a nuisance. He kept tripping, sliding his feet, falling on the ground—anything to slow them down. Waswan ended up clubbing the boy in the head to make him stop.

Gannajero stared at the northern hill again, and an unearthly fear gripped her. She couldn't seem to get her feet to move. In the dark spaces between her souls, she heard him laugh.

"Don't witch me, Child!" she snarled through gritted teeth. "That's why I left you for the wolves. I did everything I could for you, and you betrayed me!"

The faint laughter continued, rising up from the darkness that lived and breathed deep inside her.

Her slitted gaze tracked across the camp, staring at the firelit faces of hundreds of warriors. Then she trudged to her own campfire and began arranging her packs.

Four of her newly hired men were gobbling down spoonfuls of stew as fast as they could, joking between bites. Two others were digging in their packs for their cups. Three of the men were Flint warriors; two were Mountain people—including War Chief Manidos, who was a real catch; and one was a young warrior from Atotarho Village. All were slit-eyed thieves with no honor at all, loyal only to themselves and the acquisition of wealth. *Perfect.*

Gannajero knelt to tie three packs together and saw Kotin and Waswan shouldering through the camp, dragging the roped children behind them. Whimpers and coughs filtered down the line. The last child, Hawk-Face, kept stumbling to the side to vomit. How hard had Waswan hit him? She wasn't sure he was going to survive the night—and if he did, tomorrow he'd wish he hadn't. The boy staggered along with his head down and his eyes narrowed in pain. Chipmunk Teeth—just ahead of him in line—kept speaking softly to him, but Hawk-Face never replied. He looked sick to death.

Kotin stopped in front of her. "We bought two canoes. They'll be waiting for us at the river landing."

"Good." Gannajero rose to her feet and growled, "Fill your bellies and let's go. We're done here."

"Yes, Lupan. We should—" Kotin halted abruptly and stared at the men.

She followed his gaze. Two warriors stood over

the stew pot with their empty cups in their hands. Obviously they'd been just about to fill them when their gazes had been drawn to War Chief Manidos.

Manidos grimaced suddenly, then grabbed for his belly. "I don't feel...very..." He walked unsteadily to the side and started retching violently.

"What's the matter with him?" Kotin asked.

"I don't know. Maybe he—"

Another warrior stepped away from the fire, bent double, and vomited.

In less than three hundred heartbeats, all of the men who'd eaten from the pot were on their knees or writhing on the ground. Manidos had both hands around his throat, clutching it as though to strangle himself. His face had gone blue.

Gannajero swallowed hard and backed away. Kotin and Waswan retreated with her, dragging the children behind them.

Softly, Gannajero ordered, "Tear their packs off their backs. Get everything loaded in the canoes, along with the children."

"But what about the men? They're sick. Shouldn't we try to—"

"Bring only the men who didn't eat from the pot. Leave the others."

She tramped away across the camp, shouldering between laughing warriors, heading for the canoes, wondering who'd done it. A rival Trader in the camp? Or one of her own men? A traitor who wanted everything for himself? It wouldn't be the first time she'd been betrayed by one of her own.

Gannajero's gaze involuntarily slid to the northern hill. "Isn't that right, Brother?"

She had to clench her fists to keep from shaking as she hurried for the landing.

19

Koracoo clutched CorpseEye in both
hands and chased after Tutelo and the
other girl, Baji. Baji was leading Tutelo
at a dead run through the towering pines, sticking
to paths choked with brush and no wider than the
span of her own girlish shoulders, which made it
tough for adults to follow her. The girl thought like
a warrior.

Koracoo kept catching glimpses of their dresses,
and thrashed after them. She battered her way
through a thicket of nanny-bushes and charged
ahead. Behind her, she heard Sindak curse as he
followed.

"Tutelo?" she called loud enough her daughter
might hear her, but not so loud the warriors in
camp would. "Wait!"

As she ran, Koracoo shoved aside the fact that

Sindak had disobeyed her order to stay behind. Between the weave of trunks, she saw warriors moving, heading for the clearing where Gonda and the others had been. They would, of course, be gone by now, headed for the overlook hill to wait for her arrival. But the warriors would go crazy when they found their dead friends. The hunt would be on. And there were so many of them.

A horrifying cry rent the night. Koracoo jerked to look.

At the western edge of camp, a boy had broken free and was making a run for it. Two warriors chased him, cursing at the tops of their lungs. In less than twenty paces, the lead warrior tackled him and knocked him to the ground. The enraged scream split the darkness. He fought wildly, biting and kicking until the big warrior clubbed him senseless. The man dragged the boy to his feet and hauled him, stumbling drunkenly, back to the other children, where he roped him to the line.

When the boy lifted his head, Koracoo saw his face. Wrass. At least she thought it was Wrass. He'd been beaten so badly it was impossible to tell for certain.

"Koracoo, there! To the right," Sindak said.

She tugged her gaze back to the forest and glimpsed flashes of copper slipping behind the bare branches of an elderberry shrub forty paces ahead.

"Tutelo! Stop running!"

There was a moment of shocked silence; then her daughter called, "Mother?...*Mother!* Baji stop! Let me go! That's my mother!"

"It's a trick, Tutelo. We can't stop!" Baji shouted.

Koracoo leaped a fallen log, rounded the edge of the elderberries, and ran flat-out for the girls. They were now ten paces ahead. Baji was still dragging Tutelo by the hand, trying to get away, while Tutelo tugged as hard as she could to make her stop.

"Baji, let me go! Please, that's my mother!"

Koracoo called, "Tutelo, I'm here. I'm right here! Baji, please stop!"

Baji finally whirled around to look, saw Koracoo, and her eyes narrowed uncertainly. Tutelo dropped to the ground and started wrenching to get her hand free of Baji's grip. "That's my mother! It really is!"

Baji released Tutelo. As Tutelo struggled to her feet, Koracoo ran forward, grabbed Tutelo, and hugged her hard. "It's all right. I've got you."

Tutelo wept, "Oh, Mother, Mother," and buried her face in the hollow of Koracoo's throat. "Odion said you were coming. He knew you'd come for us!"

"Of course, Tutelo."

When Koracoo looked up, she saw Baji eyeing Sindak with murderous intent. The girl looked like she was on the verge of running away again.

Baji said, "You're not Standing Stone. You're Hills. You're the sworn enemy of the Standing Stone People."

"Yes, I am," Sindak replied. He slowly spread his arms as though in surrender. "But not today. My name is Sindak. I'm a friend to Tutelo's parents."

Koracoo rose to her feet, holding CorpseEye in one hand and Tutelo's fingers in the other. "Gannajero's warriors are on their way, Baji. We have to—"

Sindak glimpsed the man silently running toward them, his body flashing between the trees, but before he realized it was not Gonda or...a crazed Dawnland warrior rushed out of the trees with his war club raised, crying, "You Standing Stone filth! I'm going to kill you!" and charged.

Sindak shouted, "Koracoo, get down!"

She dove for both girls, dragged them to the ground, and covered them with her own body as Sindak raced by her to block the blow meant for Koracoo's spine. The crack of their war clubs sounded thunderous.

The enemy warrior roared, shoved Sindak away, and swung with all his might. Sindak ducked under the whirring war club, skipped sideways, and with all his strength, brought his own club around to bash the man in the back of the head.

The warrior reeled forward, weeping and mumbling. Sindak hit him again, and he collapsed to the ground.

"Come on," he said. "Let's get out of here! There's no telling how many more survivors there are out here who want to kill us."

Koracoo leaped to her feet, hauled both girls up, and ordered, "We have to run hard."

20

Three hands of time later, they crouched around a tiny fire in the dark depths of a narrow valley that cleft the long mountainous ridge. Thick plums and sumacs surrounded their camp on the northern slope and kept them hidden from prying eyes. High above, the campfires of the dead wavered through a smoky haze.

Sindak sipped his spruce needle tea and scanned the dense branches of the staghorn sumacs. Scrub trees that grew four or five times the height of a man had dark, smooth bark that reflected the multiple shadows cast by the flames. Beyond the sumacs, a thicket of thorny plums spread fifty paces in every direction. The sweet tang of rotting fruit filled the air. Most of the sharp-toothed leaves had, thankfully, been blown into the branches, leaving their small clearing almost bare.

Gonda kept feeding twigs to the blaze to keep the children and the tea warm. Despite their desperate situation, the muscles of his round face had relaxed. It made him look ten summers younger.

Sindak glanced at Koracoo. She stood five paces to the east, watching the game trail they'd followed to get here, while Towa watched the trail as it left the clearing and headed west.

None of them seemed inclined to talk, least of all, Towa. He'd been brooding over something, but they hadn't had a chance to discuss it yet.

Hehaka, Baji, Odion, and Tutelo huddled together on the opposite side of the fire from Sindak. From their expressions, Sindak suspected three of them would be standing shoulder to shoulder for the rest of their lives. All of them except Hehaka. The other children acted as if they had to watch what they said around him.

That intrigued Sindak.

He could tell that Baji was from the Flint People, and even if he hadn't known, he would have guessed Tutelo and Odion were Standing Stone—but he hadn't been able to place Hehaka's People. And the boy was...odd. His starved face resembled a trapped bat's, all ears and flat nose, with small dark eyes. The boy kept lifting his chin to sniff the air, as if scenting them to identify whether they were predator or prey.

Odion shifted, as though he'd come to a decision, and called, "Father?"

Gonda looked up. "What is it, my son?"

"Tomorrow. We have to go to Fire Cherry Camp."

Gonda tossed another twig on the flames. "I don't know where that is, Odion."

"It's less than a day's walk away." Odion blinked and stared up at the night sky. After five or six heartbeats, he wet his lips, then pointed slightly southwest. "It's there...I think. I'll find it."

Gonda exchanged a curious glance with Koracoo, who had turned to listen to the conversation. Gonda said, "I'm not sure it's safe to head west, Odion. What's at this fire cherry camp?"

Odion stiffened his spine as though to bolster his courage. "Wrass is going to meet us there. He told me. He'll be there waiting for us at dawn. He—"

"Odion?" Koracoo called, then hesitated. She turned and walked back into the clearing. Her red cape looked orange in the firelight. She knelt beside her son, and he looked at her with his whole heart in his eyes.

"Yes, Mother?"

Koracoo petted his dark hair. "Odion, forgive me. I was going to tell you tomorrow, after you'd eaten and slept, but...Wrass won't be there. He was captured by Gannajero. I watched—"

"No!" The high-pitched scream rang through the forest.

Sindak instinctively clutched his war club.

Odion leaped to his feet and stared at Koracoo as though she were a complete stranger; then he charged up the dark eastern trail like a man running for his life.

"Odion?" Gonda lunged to his feet and chased after him, calling, "Odion? Odion, no! We'll find him, but not tonight!"

Chaos erupted among the children. Baji and Tutelo stood up and started talking at once. Hehaka bent forward and put his hands over his ears, as though he couldn't bear to hear any of this.

When Gonda caught up with Odion, he grabbed the back of his shirt and shouted, "Odion, stop! We'll find Wrass. Just not tonight. Not tonight!"

Odion burst into tears and fought against Gonda's iron grip. "Let me go, Father! I have to find him *now*. You don't know. Y-You don't know what they'll d-do to him! I know. Ask Tutelo. Ask Baji and Hehaka!"

Gonda dropped to his knees and forcibly pulled Odion into his arms. Odion slammed his fists into his father's face and shoulders. "Let me go! Father, I have to find him!"

Gonda lifted his son off the ground and carried him back toward the fire.

Odion writhed and kicked, shouting, "Wrass needs me! Let me go!"

"Stop it. Odion, stop!"

Three paces from the fire, Gonda set Odion on the ground, grabbed his son's frantic fists, and held them against his chest. "Listen to me. We can't just charge into a camp filled with hundreds of warriors. None of us, including Wrass, will live through it. We need to think about it, to plan. You're a warrior now. Think! We'll go after Wrass in the morning."

Odion wailed, "You're lying! You're going to take us far away!"

"I am not lying! Tell me when I've ever lied to you?"

Odion's thin body was trembling. He swallowed hard and whispered, "...Never."

Gonda ripped open his cape and tucked his hand into his shirt over his heart. "I give you my oath as a Standing Stone warrior that I will never, *never* abandon another Standing Stone warrior being held in an enemy camp. I will find him and bring him home, even at the cost of my own life."

Sindak's gaze shifted to Koracoo. Her eyes had narrowed at Gonda's words, as though she disagreed.

Sobs shook Odion. In a choking voice, he said, "Oh, Father. Wrass saved us. If they find out what he d-did, they'll kill him!"

Gonda gripped his son by the shoulders and held him at arm's length. He solemnly stared into Odion's brimming eyes. "Then his name will be counted among the bravest warriors of our People, and I will honor him for the rest of my life. But I am not going to risk all of our lives foolishly. Do you think I should?"

Odion squeezed his eyes closed for several agonizing moments. "No."

Gonda hugged the boy tightly. "We just need time, Odion. Time to consider how to—"

"Father, I—I understand, and I won't endanger anyone else, but I'm going after Wrass and the other children at first light."

Gonda shoved back to look into Odion's brimming eyes. "Alone?"

"Yes."

The bold, confident tone of the boy's voice filled Sindak with awe. He had no idea what the child had been through, but it could not have been pleasant, and yet Odion was willing to charge back into the mouth of the beast to rescue his friend.

Gonda's eyes narrowed with pride. He softly said, "Sometime while I was away, you became a man, my son."

Baji stood up. "You're not going alone, Odion. I'm going with you."

"Me, too." Tutelo shot up beside Baji and

clenched her jaw as though daring anyone to tell her she couldn't go.

Hehaka just hung his head and stared at the ground.

Gonda turned to Koracoo. "What do you say, War Chief?"

Koracoo's gaze lingered on the determined young faces around the fire. "There are many things we must discuss first. Both of you, come and sit down."

Gonda held Odion's hand and led him back to crouch before the flames. Odion waited with wide eyes for his mother's next words.

Koracoo gently smoothed her hand over CorpseEye and said, "Sindak? Towa? I was going to wait to make plans until tomorrow when we were rested, but apparently we need to do it tonight. You must have many questions for the children. Why don't you start?"

Towa marched forward, as though he'd been eager for this moment. "Thank you, War Chief."

Towa knelt beside Sindak, and his long black braid fell over his right shoulder. He studied the children one by one and said, "We're looking for a girl who was captured in a raid fifteen days ago. Was there another little girl among you? She has seen ten summers, and has long black hair that hangs to her waist." The children frowned at each other and shook their heads. Towa continued, "Her front teeth stick out like a squir—"

"Zateri!" Tutelo cried, and Odion and Baji nodded.

"Yes, Zateri." The elation in his voice was obvious. "So she was with you?"

"Yes," Baji said. "But her hair is not long. It's cut short in mourning." She drew a line across her own hair to show how short, just below her chin.

Sindak leaned forward. "Is she all right?"

"She was alive the last time we saw her."

Towa bowed his head and exhaled in relief. He put a hand over the sacred pendant beneath his cape. "Then we must continue on, War Chief, though we will understand if you want to take these children to safety first."

Odion whirled to stare at Koracoo. "I'm going with them, Mother."

Koracoo stood for several moments, staring out into the darkness, before she heaved a sigh and said, "It's too dangerous to take the children with us. Dangerous for them as well as for us. They'll distract us and slow us down. I am inclined to send them back—"

"No, Mother!" Odion cried.

"I agree," Towa interrupted. "Someone must get these children to safety, while the rest of us continue on the trail."

"Towa's right," Sindak said. "If we aren't on Gannajero's trail at dawn, we may lose it forever. I suggest that you, War Chief, and Gonda take the children home, while Towa and I go after Zateri."

Tears silently ran down Odion's cheeks. "Zateri isn't the only one. You have to free *all* of the children. *All of them!* How are you going to do that? You need us. We know Gannajero's meeting places, and how she hides her trails. We know how she thinks, and what her men look like. You don't know any of these things!"

Sindak's brows lowered. The boy was right. Having that kind of knowledge might make the difference between life and death. "If you can describe her men to us, we—"

"No." Odion shook his head. "You have to take me with you."

"You have to take *us* with you," Baji said.

Sindak frowned. That little girl had a gaze that could lance right through a man's vitals. She was a born clan matron or warrior. He'd hate to have to stand before her in a council meeting ten summers from now. On the other hand, looking into those eyes across a bow wasn't going to be a pretty sight either.

"My inclination," Koracoo said, "is to send the children to Atotarho Village with Sindak, while we continue searching for the other children."

Shocked, Sindak objected, "But you need me the most, War Chief. I'm the best tracker, and I—"

Gonda said, "If any of us has to go, it's you. You bring out the worst in people."

"I bring out the worst in *you*. Let's look at facts: I'm not the one who's spent the past half-moon staring at his feet with his war club dragging the ground. And despite your woeful conduct, I've been nice!"

"That's what you call being nice? You obviously don't grasp the problem."

Sindak scowled and said, "War Chief, Gonda is the expendable member of this party. He should take the children to the closest Standing Stone village, and remain there until we come for him."

All of the children had started to whimper and sniffle. Koracoo glanced around the fire. "Towa? You've been quiet."

Towa looked up from where he'd been glaring at his hands. "This entire discussion is irrelevant to me."

Koracoo's brows arched. "Why?"

"Well, you're not going to like this, Koracoo, but our chief ordered us to obey all of your orders—except one."

Koracoo's chin lifted. "Which one?"

"He said that if you ever ordered us to stop searching for his daughter, we were to go on without you." Towa watched her hands tighten around CorpseEye and added, "I'm sorry, but neither Sindak nor I have the luxury of retreating with the children. We must find our chief's daughter and bring her home."

Her gaze slid to Gonda, probably considering Sindak's proposal, and Gonda suddenly straightened. "Koracoo, think about this. You're asking one man to sneak through a war-torn country with three children and miraculously get them to safety. With two of us, it might be possible. But not one man."

Towa said, "He may be right. There are thousands of warriors on the trails."

Gonda added, "It's regrettable, but the children are probably safer traveling with us—"

"—right into the jaws of death," Sindak finished for him. "Really, War Chief, this is silly. None of us is safe if we're stumbling over children while we're trying to draw back our bows. Send Gonda away with the children."

Gonda leaned forward and gave Sindak a smile.

Sindak waited for him to speak, and when he didn't, asked, "Why are you looking at me like that?"

"I was imagining your head in a stewpot."

Scary. Sindak could suddenly see his own boiled eyes staring up at him.

"Well, then, there's another reason. If he's planning on murdering me, I'd rather not have him here."

Gonda laughed softly. "Of course not. Without me to keep watch on you, you'd be free to spend all of your time excitedly following your minuscule erection from one pipe stem to another—"

"Enough." Koracoo's eyes narrowed. She glanced back and forth between them for a time before she said, "I've made my decision."

They all fell silent.

She squared her shoulders. "We're taking the children with us, and leaving long before dawn. I want to be at the river landing just before sunrise."

"Very well." Towa nodded.

Sindak had assumed the children would cheer. They did not.

The silence stretched. The children glanced at each other, but there wasn't even a smile—just a sober realization that tomorrow would carry them right back into Gannajero's lair.

Only Hehaka reacted. He said, "You're taking me home?"

Wrenching sadness filled Koracoo's eyes. "Finish your cups of tea and get to sleep. We must all be well rested."

The children drained their cups and curled up around the fire without another word.

Koracoo added, "Gonda, take Towa's guard

position. Sindak, I'll wake you in three hands of time to take my watch."

"Yes, War Chief."

Gonda and Koracoo trotted in opposite directions and took up their positions guarding the trail.

21

Sindak threw another handful of twigs onto the low flames and glanced at Towa. His black eyes and straight nose had a pinched look. He fiddled with the hem of his buckskin cape, creasing it between his fingers.

"You've been brooding since we left the warriors' camp. What's wrong?"

Towa tilted his head uncertainly. "I'm not sure about this, so don't fall down and kick your heels in a fit."

Sindak sat back. "What?"

Towa spread his hands, palms up. "When Gonda and I were lying on the overlook hill waiting for you and Koracoo, I thought I saw... someone...maybe two people...down in that camp."

"Two people?" The expression on Towa's face had made Sindak go still. "People you knew?"

Towa rested his hands on his knees. "I'm sure I'm mistaken, all right?"

"You've already said that. Who were they?"

Towa grimaced. "Well, the one I really saw looked like Akio. He was—"

"Don't be ridiculous." Sindak laughed. "He's too fat to have waddled this far."

Towa jerked a nod and let out a breath. "I'm sure I'm wrong."

"Why would he be here? After Atotarho made the deal with Koracoo, the elders decided not to send out the war party, so there's no reason—"

A hot tide swelled in Sindak's veins and rushed through his body. The logical conclusion struck him with the force of a war club to his head. "No," he said. "I don't believe it."

Towa ran a hand through his black hair. "I don't either. But why else would he be here?"

"Akio?" Sindak hissed incredulously. "The traitor?"

Towa didn't say anything. He just tossed another clump of twigs onto the tiny blaze to keep it burning. A bed of red coals had built up. It would continue to warm them for a couple of hands of time.

Sindak said, "You said there were two people you recognized. Who was the other?"

Towa ground his teeth for a long moment. His jaw moved beneath his tanned cheek. "He was an old man with gray hair, being carried on a litter by men I did not know. I never saw him step off the litter, but he wore a black cape with white ornaments—maybe circlets of human skull."

Sindak blinked. "Could you see his face?"

"No, I was too far away."

"Well, that's not much evidence then. Many people have black capes with white ornaments." But Towa had seen Atotarho's cape many times. He probably would not mistake it, even at a distance. It was a frightening possibility. In the back of Sindak's thoughts, Gonda's voice hissed: *You actually believe Atotarho sent you along with us to help rescue his daughter.* "And even if it's true, there's nothing we can do about it tonight."

"You're right."

Towa rose and went to his pack by the tree to pull out his blanket. He threw it over his shoulder and walked back to the fire. After wrapping up in it, he stretched out on his back, but didn't close his eyes. He stared up at the dark night sky.

Sindak ground his teeth for a time, then whispered, "Don't go to sleep yet. There's something I want to discuss with you."

"What?"

Sindak glanced at the children; then he swiveled around and, barely audible, said, "I almost fainted when I first heard Gonda call his son's name."

Towa's bushy brows drew together. "Why?"

"Do you remember the night I was late getting to the fork in the trail?"

"The night you were chased by the warriors?"

Sindak nodded. "I swear the man wearing the herringbone sandals was calling a name: *Odion.*"

Towa shrugged. "That doesn't mean anything. There are probably dozens of Standing Stone boys named that."

"But why would a warrior chasing *me* call that name?"

Towa braced himself up on one elbow. "Are you suggesting that he wasn't chasing you? He was chasing Koracoo's son?"

"I don't know what I'm suggesting. Maybe he was. Or maybe he was trying to tell me that Odion was close, and I should follow him. I don't know, but—"

The pretty little girl, Tutelo, sat up and peered at them with large, dark eyes. A halo of black tangles framed her face. She hissed, "It was Shago-niyoh. The Child. He's been calling Odion for days."

"You have ears like a bat," Sindak said. "Go back to sleep."

"It was Shago-niyoh," she repeated.

"Who's Shago-niyoh?" Towa asked.

Tutelo eased away from the other exhausted children and crawled toward them. She got on her knees beside Towa and whispered, "He's a human False Face."

Towa suppressed a smile. "Is he? Did you see him with your own eyes?"

"Yes," she answered firmly. "He's tall and has a crooked nose and a long black cape."

Teasing, Towa asked, "He doesn't wear herringbone-weave sandals, does he? That would answer a lot of our questions."

In a deadly earnest voice, Tutelo replied, "He wears sandals, but I've never seen the weave."

A chill tingled Sindak's spine. The little girl was utterly serious. He glanced at Towa. His friend had a skeptical expression on his face. Sindak shifted to prepare himself, and asked, "So... this Shago-niyoh has spoken to you?"

"Oh, yes, he came to visit us many times when we were slaves. He was trying to help us escape."

As though half-amused, but a little worried, too, Towa said, "Does he wear one of these?" He reached into his cape and pulled out the gorget. It was so big it rested like a magnificent shell platter on his chest.

Tutelo moved closer and reached out to touch it. "No, but...this is beautiful. Look at the shooting stars! Who made it?"

"Well, our legends say that two of these were created during the Beginning Time. The human False Face who is to come will..." His voice dwindled to nothing. He was staring over Sindak's shoulder.

Sindak jerked around, expecting to see a war party rushing them.

Instead, Hehaka was sitting up. His mouth opened and closed, as though he couldn't speak. Finally his finger snaked from beneath his cape, and he croaked, "What—what is that?"

"It's a sacred gorget," Towa explained. "It chronicles the story of the death of Horned Serpent. There's no reason to be afraid. It's just a carved shell."

Hehaka shivered. "My father had one like that...I think."

"Your father?"

Hehaka shook his head. "Yes, I think that's who the man was. I'm not sure. I remember almost nothing about my family or village. But I remember that. It used to swing above my eyes when the man bent over to kiss me at night." He hugged himself as though the memory hurt. "The last time I saw it, I was four summers. That's when I became Ganna-jero's slave."

As though disparate puzzle pieces were being pulled together from across vast distances, Sindak's heart thundered. "What's your nation? Are you from the Hills People?"

Hehaka lifted his nose and sniffed the air, as though scenting them again. "I don't know. Why?"

Towa started to answer, but Sindak cut him off. "No reason," he said. "Go back to sleep, both of you. We're going to run your legs off tomorrow."

Hehaka reluctantly curled up on his side, and Tutelo crawled back beside her brother. But instead of closing her eyes, she kept staring at them.

Sindak positioned himself so that his back was to her and his body blocked Towa from her view, then whispered, "It's not possible, is it?"

Towa gestured lamely with his hand. "It was seven summers ago. Why not?" Towa gave him a knowing look, stretched out on the ground, and pulled his blanket up to his chin. "Sleep, Sindak. You're going to need it."

Sindak exhaled hard and got to his feet. "Later," he said.

He walked up the trail to the east. Only Koracoo's head moved when she saw him coming. Her black eyes fixed questioningly on him.

Sindak stopped a pace away and folded his arms tightly over his chest. "War Chief, there's something I need to discuss with you."

22

Gonda's gaze shifted between watching the western trail and watching Sindak and Koracoo. They spoke in low, ominous voices twenty paces away. Talking about what? Sindak was supposed to be asleep. Everyone else was dreaming by the fire. Though Towa kept flopping and twitching, the children looked innocent and peaceful.

Gonda checked the western trail again. The wind had blown a thick cloud of smoke over the top of them. There was no light except for that cast by the tiny blaze, and it flickered weakly, on the verge of going out. He couldn't see more than thirty paces up the trail. If he was going to stop any intruders, he'd have to hear them, not see them. He tried to concentrate on the sounds of the night. Wind sighed through the plum trees, and the few shriveled fruits that clung to the branches rattled. Limbs creaked. Old leaves rustled as they whipped around the forest.

Koracoo's soft steps patted the trail behind him.

He turned and could see the tightness around her dark eyes.

Sindak walked back to the fire and rolled up in his blanket near Towa.

Before Koracoo stopped, he said, "What's wrong?"

She swung CorpseEye up and rested the club on her shoulder.

After she'd ground her teeth for several moments, she said, "Towa thought he saw Atotarho in the warriors' camp tonight."

"Impossible. He was mistaken." Gonda examined her face. "But...you don't think so, do you?"

"Hehaka told Sindak that his long-lost father owned a gorget like the one Towa wears."

Gonda shook his head lightly, trying to figure out where she was going. "Who's his father?"

Koracoo's gaze lanced straight through him. "The boy is eleven. He was captured when he was four."

"So, seven summers ago..." He regripped his war club. "What?"

"Sindak told me that's when Atotarho's only son was captured in a raid."

Gonda felt suddenly as though he were floating. "Are you saying...wait...I don't understand. Are you suggesting that Gannajero is targeting his family? First his son? Now his daughter? Why would she do that?"

"I don't know, but I have an idea." She turned toward where Sindak lay, rolled in his blanket by the fire. "Let's go ask some questions."

Sindak heard them coming and sat up with his blanket still draped over his shoulders. He rubbed his eyes. "I'm listening."

Koracoo knelt in front of him. "When we were in your village, Atotarho told us a story. He said that when he was a child, his older brother and sister were captured in a raid. Do you know anything about that?"

Sindak shook his head. "No. However, everyone in our village knows that when he was twenty summers, his younger brother and sister, twins, were captured in a raid."

Gonda glanced at Koracoo. Her eyes had started to blaze. "He lied to us. Koracoo...he lied. What's he hiding?"

"Sindak, how old were the twins?" Koracoo asked.

Sindak blinked his tired eyes. "Eight summers, I think. It was devastating for his clan. If she'd lived, his sister would have become the most powerful clan matron in our village."

"What would have happened to Atotarho?" Gonda asked.

"As is customary, he would have married and moved to his wife's village."

"And," Gonda said softly, "the gorget that Towa now wears would have passed to his sister when she became clan matron."

Sindak's gaze suddenly darted between Koracoo and Gonda. "Are you suggesting that maybe she did not die?"

Towa had wakened and lay on his back, listening with his dark eyes narrowed. He said, "If she's alive, why hasn't she returned home to claim her rightful position among our people?"

Koracoo's face suddenly went slack, as though a horrifying thought had occurred to her. She slowly rose to her feet and stared down at Sindak. "Maybe that's why Towa has that gorget. He's supposed to deliver it to her."

Gonda, Sindak, and Towa gazed at her in silence.

Across the fire, Odion sat up. He didn't say a word. He just stared at them as though he finally understood something.

23

Green water had been rippling by all night, scalloped here and there with starlit foam that spun off the paddle strokes of the warriors. Gannajero sat in the bow of the lead canoe, snarling at anyone who dared to speak to her.

Wrass, and three children he did not know, rode in the second canoe. Four warriors dipped their paddles and drove their canoe forward. They were moving swiftly, heading south into the lands of the People Who Separated, a group of rebels who'd broken away from the People of the Dawnland many summers before. The banks were thick with dark green holly. Just beyond them, leafless birches and elms grew. They cast cool, wavering shadows across the leaden river.

Wrass repositioned his hot cheek on the gunwale. His headache caused tears to constantly leak from his eyes and silently fall into the river. Before Gannajero had separated them, Zateri had thrust strips of birch bark into his hands and told him to chew them. They'd helped a little. When he could keep them down long enough. He'd thrown up so often that his throat was raw and swollen. And he kept having blackouts—long periods where he couldn't remember anything.

A warrior waddled down the canoe, making it rock from side to side. Water sloshed, and white-caps bobbed away. The man knelt beside Wrass. "You let them catch you, didn't you?" he hissed. "To distract them from hunting the other children? You're a stupid boy. You could be halfway home by now."

It took a gigantic amount of strength to lift his eyes to the man. "Who are you?"

The stars' gleam cast a pewter glow over the warrior's pudgy, florid face. He'd taken off every ornament and piece of clothing that would have identified his clan or People, and wore a plain elkhide cape and black leggings. Wrass tried to focus on him, but he was blurry, his face striped with the dark shadows of the passing trees.

"Gannajero says if you're not better by the time we make camp tonight, I have to kill you." He sounded unhappy about it.

A smile touched Wrass' lips. "That must be hard...for a coward like you."

The warrior brutally punched Wrass in the belly, and he scrambled forward to hold his head over the gunwale and vomit into the river. Nothing came up, but he couldn't stop gagging.

"Just wait, boy. If you think it's bad now, when I tell Gann—"

"Akio!" Kotin called. "You lazy fool, what are you doing? Get back to your paddle."

The fat warrior glanced at Kotin, then leaned over Wrass and growled, "I know you were the one who poisoned the stew, boy. I saw you by the pot. I've just been waiting to tell Gannajero." He tramped away and picked up his paddle again.

The wrenching convulsions continued until the edges of his vision started to go gray and fluttery...and Wrass...he...he was...

Vaguely, he felt his body sink into the canoe, and knew his head rested on soft packs.

24

Later that night, just before Koracoo was supposed to wake Sindak to take over her sentry position, Gonda filled his lungs with the damp, smoky air and walked in her direction.

As frost settled over the clearing, the fallen plums resembled a field of small white river rocks. He tiptoed around the fire, which had burned down to a glistening bed of coals, trying not to wake anyone. Koracoo watched his approach with worried eyes. Every twig on the bare branches behind her was tipped in silver.

Gonda stopped a pace away and gripped his war club in both hands, holding it in front of him like the locking plank of a door that should never be opened.

"What is it, Gonda?"

His hands hardened to fists. "Please, just listen. Don't say anything."

She spread her feet, preparing herself.

When he began, his voice was low and deep. "You'd sent Coter and Hagnon out to scout that morning. They came back at dusk. Coter was wounded. Hagnon dragged him through the front gate and told me that the attacking warriors had let him through. They thought it was all a big joke... because it didn't matter what they told me." Her eyes narrowed, and he looked away. He couldn't bear to see the cold, impenetrable wall go up. He plunged on. "Hagnon told me he suspected there were at least one thousand warriors—"

She shifted to reposition her feet.

"—spread out through the forest, aligned for waves of attacks. I kept going to our elders, begging them to let me create some kind of diversion that would allow a few of our old people and children to escape, but they refused. They told me to keep fighting."

He expelled a breath. He dared not look at her now—not until he'd finished. "Two hands of time later the palisade was on fire in fifty places, riddled with holes; enemy warriors were crawling in, swarming all over like rats in a corn bin. I ran through the longhouses, gathered all the children and elders who were still able to run, and led them outside with one hundred warriors at my back. We

—we fought hard, Koracoo." His voice was shaking. "Gods, it was terrible. But...some...a few...escaped."

She didn't say a word.

Gonda girded himself, and lifted his eyes to look at her quiet, tormented face.

"Gonda," she whispered with difficulty. "I should never have split our forces and gone out that morning." A sob spasmed her chest. She forced it down. "If I'd kept all six hundred of our warriors in the village, not even one thousand could have breached our walls. We could have saved...so many."

She turned away, and her shoulders shook as though there was an earthquake inside her.

For a moment, he just stood there. Afraid. Then he said, "Blessed gods. Forgive me, Koracoo. If I hadn't been drowning in my own guilt, I would have seen that you..."

He stepped forward and pulled her against him. How long had it been since she'd let him hold her? For a few blessed moments, he enjoyed the sensation of her body against his. "Don't look back," he said. "If we start looking back, it's all we'll be able to do."

Slowly, Koracoo's arms went around his back, and she clutched him so hard her arms shuddered.

"You lied to me, didn't you?" he asked.

"About what?"

"You told me your greatest fear was the same as

mine, that you'd fail to protect your family...but that's not true, is it?"

She hesitated. "No."

"No," he softly repeated. "Of course not. You are war chief. Your greatest duty is to keep your village safe."

He could see it all so clearly now. The fear that tied her soul to her body was that she would fail to protect her People. In her heart, she must be swimming toward a shore she couldn't even see.

Gonda kissed her hair, and it was as if a gentle, cool hand were stealing over his wounded souls. He could feel the quiet hush of the autumn evening in the mountains and smell the pleasant fragrance of burning plum branches. The peaceful faces of the children reflected the fluttering firelight. They would never be able to go home. They no longer had a home to go to.

He hugged Koracoo tighter. He didn't want to think of that now. All he wanted was a place where they could lick their wounds, a quiet place to heal, and try to imagine a future.

Against his shoulder, Koracoo said, "Tomorrow, we'll find the rest of the children."

He took a deep breath.

"Yes," he answered. "We will."

A LOOK AT BOOK THREE:
THE DAWN COUNTRY

The epic tale that began in *People Of The Longhouse* continues in Part three of the amazing Peacemaker's Tale series from *New York Times* bestselling authors and archaeologists Kathleen O'Neal Gear and W. Michael Gear.

War Chief Koracoo and Deputy Gonda of the Standing Stone People have successfully rescued their children, Odion and Tutelo, from the fearsome witch, Gannajero. But Odion's friend, Wrass is still held captive in Gannajero's camp, along with several other children, and Koracoo and Gonda are determined to save them all.

This time, Koracoo and Gonda have allies: a battle-weary Mohawk war chief and a healer who have also lost children to Gannajero. These bitter enemies must learn to trust one another and find common ground.

Will they be able to put their differences aside and rescue the children before they are sold and carried off to distant villages, lost to their families and homes forever?

AVAILABLE JUNE 2024

ABOUT W. MICHAEL GEAR

W. Michael Gear is a *New York Times, USA Today,* and international bestselling author of sixty novels. With close to eighteen million copies of his books in print worldwide, his work has been translated into twenty-nine languages.

Gear has been inducted into the Western Writers Hall of Fame and the Colorado Authors' Hall of Fame—as well as won the Owen Wister Award, the Golden Spur Award, and the International Book Award for both Science Fiction and Action Suspense Fiction. He is also the recipient of the Frank Waters Award for lifetime contributions to Western writing.

Gear's work, inspired by anthropology and archaeology, is multilayered and has been called compelling, insidiously realistic, and masterful. Currently, he lives in northwestern Wyoming with his award-winning wife and co-author, Kathleen O'Neal Gear, and a charming sheltie named, Jake.

ABOUT KATHLEEN O'NEAL GEAR

Kathleen O'Neal Gear is a *New York Times* bestselling author of fifty-seven books and a national award-winning archaeologist. The U.S. Department of the Interior has awarded her two Special Achievement awards for outstanding management of America's cultural resources.

In 2015 the United States Congress honored her with a Certificate of Special Congressional Recognition, and the California State Legislature passed Joint Member Resolution #117 saying, "The contributions of Kathleen O'Neal Gear to the fields of history, archaeology, and writing have been invaluable..."

In 2021 she received the Owen Wister Award for lifetime contributions to western literature, and in 2023 received the Frank Waters Award for "a body of work representing excellence in writing and storytelling that embodies the spirit of the American West."

Made in the USA
Columbia, SC
14 August 2024

40437381R00138